SHENANIGANS

The unofficial history of Monroe County, Iowa

TONY HUMESTON

PBL Limited
Ottumwa, Iowa

SHENANIGANS: An Unofficial History of Monroe County, Iowa
by Tony Humeston

10 9 8 7 6 5 4 3 2 1

ISBN 1-892689-70 -7

ISBN 13: 978-1-892689-70-2

Photo credits: Photographs and illustrations from the author's personal collection: pages 4, 7, 8, 9, 10, 21, 39, 42, 81, 116. Photograph page 40: from the collection of Molly Richards; used with permission. Photograph on page 70: from the Michael W. Lemberger Collection; used with permission. Illustrations by Michael W. Lemberger: pages 12, 25, 30, 32, 51, and 71; copyright Michael W. Lemberger, used with permission.

Printed in the United States of America

Copies of this book are available from PBL Limited. See page 120 for details on ordering by mail, or visit our website at www.pbllimited.com for more information and to read samples.

Many of the incidents in this collection are ones I was involved in. Naturally, "The Sting" happened before my time, but I heard it from enough credible people to believe it to be true. Other stories have been handed down through families in Monroe County for generations until some of the details have been lost; I've retold them as I imagine they happened.

I have skipped other incidents to avoid embarrassing people I haven't seen for years. Besides, I don't want to be sued. Other adventures were too short or too disjointed to pass muster. Some things Royce Donohoe and I did were outrageous or stupid, depending on how you look at it. Our antics kept both of our Guardian Angels busy.

For instance, one time Royce and I stood on my parents' garage roof during an electrical storm telling each other that whoever jumped first was chicken. One beautifully-awesome bolt just about got us. There was a clap of thunder, lightning splintered the sky, and an oval ball of fire flashed almost overhead. (At least it seemed almost overhead.) Eight curved tentacles came out of the sides of the thing and made it look like a huge spider. It left a strange smell in the air – I later learned it was ozone. Scared? We were almost glued to the garage roof in fear.

My mother looked out the back porch window and saw us cowering up there with this strange lightning bolt above us. She almost lost it. At her rather urgent requests, we became unglued and jumped down. Mom was mad a long time over that one.

This book was fun to write. I hope you enjoy it.

Tony Humeston
Albia, Iowa
December, 2008

GROWING UP IN THE FORTIES

My grandfather, Dwight S. Humeston, came from Wayne County to Albia in 1905. Armed with a business degree from Gem City Business College in Elgin, Illinois, he landed a job with Zook Furniture and Undertaking, which operated out of the building where the Skean Block is now. Grandfather married well, tying the knot with Ed Whited's middle daughter. One of the little coincidences of life is that Maggie Morrison, who later became my other grandmother, operated the catering service for the happy occasion.

In about 1912, grandfather opened his own business and it prospered or declined depending upon the ebb and flow of the economy. His marriage produced three sons: Dwight, Dan, and Dick. In the meantime, Maggie Morrison married Joe Bates, a rural mail carrier in Melrose. Their union was blessed with sons Maurice, Jim, Bill, and daughter, Mary. Mary Bates married Dwight Humeston. They were my parents.

I was raised across the street from the funeral home on South Clinton street. My buddy, Royce Donohoe, lived next door. The biggest influence on our early years had to have been World War Two. There were some anxious times in the early part of the war. I'd hear adults talk about us losing the Philippines or getting beaten by Rommel in Northern Africa. But they would usually end the conversation saying something like, "Those dumb bastards are going to be sorry they jumped us."

We prayed at home, in church, and in school for victory and the safe return of our soldiers. Little flags with a star hung from front windows to designate that a man from that house was in the military. And when a

Dwight Sutton Humeston

hometown soldier died, past enmities would be forgotten. The people, all dirt poor by today's standards, would come together like an injured family.

Meat was rationed, and there wasn't a squirrel or rabbit in town. My folks had a lot-sized garden and my mother canned vegetables. There were fruit trees in every yard, probably left over from depression days. Everybody had a big garden and raised chickens or rabbits. There wasn't much money. The movies cost a dime and we didn't even consider going. Evening times my folks would sit on the porch swing and talk to passing people. A team of horses or a man on horseback was a common sight. In fact, O'Reilly's Auto Parts Store and Felton's Welding Shop were blacksmith shops in the early forties.

We had neither television nor air-conditioning. Radio and board games were our evening sources of entertainment. We listened to *The Lone Ranger*, *Fibber McGee and Mollie*, and others. A good one was *The Shadow*. It starts off with, "Who knows what evil lurks in the hearts of men? The Shadow knows." *The Inner Sanctum* was another scary one. It started with a squeaking door and a low chuckle.

Over the years, a whole platoon of us boys learned our Latin prayers from Pearl on Father Heinen's back porch. Pearl must have thought that busy hands are happy hands because we snapped green beans while we memorized and recited the Confiteor. In time, we passed muster and were sent out on the altar with maybe a dozen other boys.

We walked down South Clinton Street to the old Grant School building. Discipline was strict and swift, as I was to find out. Recesses were a blast. Kids made their own fun. Between fights, we boys shot marbles. The games most played were Bull Ring, Follows-up and Poison-hole. Sometimes we traded marbles. Commies (home made clay marbles) weren't worth much. Glassies were so-so. Agates and steelies (ball bearings) commanded the best prices.

The girls played on the west side of the school. They jumped rope and played jacks, as far as I know. Two girls would hold on to opposite ends of a twelve-foot rope. They would swing it in a large loop and chant:

"Apples, pears, peaches, plums,
Tell us when your birthday comes!"
"January-February-March-April-May-June-July-August-September-October-November-December!"

as fast as they could utter the words. The girl was supposed to jump in on her birthday month.

Another chant was:

"All together girls,
  It's fine weather, girls,
When your birthday comes,
Please jump in!"

Then the rope swingers would recite the months and the girl jump in.

Winter times we boys played Fox and Geese and had snowball wars. I have no idea what the girls did. Winter coats were mostly hand-me-downs and patched. At the war's end, there was a plethora of remodeled military coats among the kids. You could see where the unit patches and stripes had been on the shoulders. I don't recall anybody making fun of someone else's clothes.

About the fifth grade, things started changing in my lifestyle. People farther up in the family hierarchy decided I could carry folding chairs before and after wakes. The furniture store always needed dusting. I started going to work regularly after school in about the eighth grade. It didn't hurt me a bit. Best thing that ever happened to me. Summers were still free for me to be a boy.

That's the mix we were raised in—God, school, and work—Royce, Sonny, and dozens more. We started kindergarten the same year and graduated from high school together. All are scattered now. My buddy Royce is dead and his ashes rest in Saint Mary's Cemetery perhaps a stone's throwaway from Father Heinen's grave.

SINCE YOU ASKED

In my lifetime, I have probably been asked a thousand times why the funeral business and the furniture business are one business operation, especially in county seats. Here's why:

During the Civil War, men who took care of the dead Union soldiers were called undertakers. They wore black business suits and tall black hats. Most owned a black rig and a team of matched black horses. They got their buggies as close to the front line as they dared and offered, for a price, to embalm the dead soldier and send his body home in a casket. The sheer number of corpses allowed arterial embalming to be perfected. That meant a slain Yankee could be shipped home and his body displayed without a terrible stench.

Before a battle, the infantrymen would make a business deal with the undertaker. The soldier's name and address was written on a playing card and fastened to his shirt. Soldiers are a superstitious lot and that's how the Ace of Spades became known as the death card. After the battle, if the undertaker could find the slain soldier, he embalmed

Horse-drawn
funeral coach
which belonged
to the Humeston
Funeral Home

the body, casketed it, and wrote the family for shipping instructions. If the body couldn't be located, the undertaker sent the funeral money to the family with his condolences. Most Yankee soldiers carried a five-dollar gold piece in their boot. In the event he got captured, five dollars would buy his freedom from any Confederate. The undertakers always sent the five-dollar gold piece home with the body. These actions earned them the reputation of great honesty.

Wayne Parsons, who married my cousin, Diane, told me the following Civil War story. His great-grand parents, who farmed in Lee County, had two sons in the war. They came home from town one afternoon and found the casketed bodies of both of them on their front porch. Sometimes the word doesn't get through.

During the era of the 1840—1870's, the cabinetmaker also made wooden coffins. With the coming of the railroads into the Midwest, and the rise of manufacturing in the East, the cabinetmaker evolved into a furniture store that also sold factory-made caskets. People started to demand embalmed bodies. The furniture merchant became an embalmer and added a funeral parlor to his store. He soon learned there's a lot more money in funerals than the furniture business. So, between funerals he sold what furniture he could.

With the shrinking of population in county seats and the explosions of mass advertising in the cities, the economic pie grew smaller. Nowadays, government controls, taxes, and inventory control make running two businesses almost impossible for a mom-and-pop operation. There's a saying about furniture/funeral home owners that goes like this: "The first generation builds it, the second one lives off it, and the third one sells it."

THE STING

This story has been in the family for three generations and needs to be told.

Ed Whited was my great-grandfather. He was a horse trader and operated a livery stable just north of the Falvey Lumberyard. Whited was a heavily muscled man with a handlebar mustache, and clever from all accounts. Memories of childhood poverty stoked fires in him. His sometime partner and longtime friend was Paddeen O'Horo. O'Horo was a smaller man with a shock of red hair and an infectious smile. An impulsive Celt, he loved life and hated Englishmen equally. The two men were gentlemen, respected for their business acumen and honesty.

During the Boer War (1901-1903), the British were buying horses. Southern Iowa was horse country in those days. A certain Major Browning of the British Army came through this area every six months buying horses. On a previous trip, he had lied to Whited and O'Horo and skinned them in a deal. The partners were furious, but patient.

In due time Major Browning contacted the two men again and said he would soon be in the area to buy horses. All animals had to be fourteen to fifteen hands high to satisfy

8   W. E. Whited Livery stable, located on Clinton Street in Albia, pictured in about 1899.

Her Majesty's Army. O'Horo knew where there were sixty-four horses—that's four boxcar loads in those days. Unfortunately none of them was tall enough to meet the army's requirements. But the undersize horses could be bought for a song. Great Britain was paying top dollar for horses, and the two men had a score to settle. Hmm.

The partners telegraphed Browning and he arranged to stop in Albia.

On the day of the deal, the partners had their undersize horses in the corrals that used to lie west of the old C.B.&Q. Depot. It was a pleasant summer morning, and a south breeze kicked up dust devils on the trampled dirt. When the coal-burning steam engine huffed into the station and wheezed to a stop, the penned horses spooked, milled in tight groups and kicked at the corral railings. Major Browning, resplendent in his military uniform, dismounted from the train and greeted the partners effusively. Behind him the railroad men were opening boxcar doors and setting up a loading ramp.

As the three men walked to the corral, Browning glanced at the horses and scanned the set-up. The corral was thirty feet away from the boxcars. Midway between the train and the horses stood the measuring post. Major Browning strutted over to the measuring post and produced a folding carpenter's ruler. With pursed lips, he measured the height of the post. "Sixty inches from top to bottom," he rumbled and his moustache fluttered. "That's fifteen hands."

"Yes, we set the post this morning, Sir. We thought it might move things along," O'Horo said.

William Edgar Whited
(1854-1931)

"Excellent planning, gentlemen. I like that kind of thinking," Major Browning said.

Whited nodded in approval and O'Horo kicked at a desiccated horse dropping.

Major Browning took his pocketknife and cut a notch in the measuring post a hand span below the top. "That notch is at fourteen hands. All horses' withers must pass between the post's top and the notch. Agreed?"

Whited nodded again and O'Horo looked for something else to kick.

"Here's the drill: the animals will be led past the measuring post in groups of three. I will verify your count and check each horse for height. Any questions?" Major Browning huffed his mustache and looked from one partner to the other.

Silence.

"Tut! Tut! Let's get about our business. O'Horo, have the men tie three horses together and bring them past me."

"Major, the horses took an awful fright from the train's infernal racket. Why don't we let them settle down somewhat and you and I go have a drink?" O'Horo suggested.

"Capitol idea, Paddeen," Browning agreed. The two got in Whited's buggy and went uptown.

While the two men were off refreshing themselves, SOMEONE sawed four inches off the top of the measuring post and smeared dirt on the raw wood. A notch was cut a hand span down from the new top.

When the men return an hour later, the corralled horses are calmed down. O'Horo ties Whited's horse to a hitching ring and hurries to help the major. On his third attempt, the major grasps O'Horo's hand and struggles out of the buggy. Supported by O'Horo, the Englishman reels to the measuring post. Major Browning waves his right hand vaguely and the counting and grading begins.

One gets the picture of Whited sweating in a dark three-piece suit and bowler hat. O'Horo, his thick red hair twisting in the Iowa breeze, is a model of Christian charity as he holds Major Browning perpendicular. Browning squints owlishly at the measuring post. The first horse is led past with a rope tied to his tail and to the neck of the second one. Number two horse has a rope tied to his tail and the neck of the third. Browning huffs his mustache and waves them on. They are led up the ramp and into the boxcar.

In a short time, the four boxcars are full. Gold coin and handshakes are exchanged. The Major is happy; Whited and O'Horo are delighted. They pour Browning onto the train and almost dance back to Whited's buggy. The score is even. England: 1 – Whited and O'Horo: 1.

THE TALKING CROW

In 1943, when I was eight years old, Royce Donohoe and I, accompanied by his black dog who someone with great imagination had named Midnight, were exploring in the creek right south of Oakwood Cemetery. We came out of the creek bed at the west end of the cemetery. After daring each other, we tight-rope-walked on a pipe that stretched across a deep ditch and entered a lane that runs just west of the cemetery. We flushed a crow that flew ahead of us and slammed into a windfall. Stunned, the bird fell to the ground. In a quicksilver of time, we were on him.

"What are we going to do with the crow?" Royce asked.

I can see it all yet. Royce was wearing a red and white plaid shirt. He held the crow in his right arm, next to his chest. With his other hand, he stroked the bird's head. The crow seemed happy. I bet Midnight was confused.

"This crow is going to make us rich," I declared.

"How's that?" Royce asked and petted the crow's head.

"Everybody knows the crow is the smartest bird in the whole world. If you split a crow's tongue, it can talk just like us," I told him.

"You sure?" Royce seemed a little reluctant. He had been in on my schemes before.

"Of course. I read all about it," I said. "Once the crow's speaking, we'll put him in a cage, and travel all around charging people a nickel to talk to him. Just think of the money we'll make."

"How are we going to split its tongue?"

"We'll go to my house and get my mother's scissors," I told him. "Nothing to it."

"Let's go," Royce said and visions of riches must have danced in his head.

We walked through the cemetery and cut down alleys to my house. As we went, my mind seethed, sorting out the details. My mother had a sewing room in our house complete with bolts of material and a Singer sewing machine. I was forbidden to go into the room. She had showed me a pair of sharp scissors and instructed me not to even touch them. The war was on and there were no more scissors to be had at any price.

© Michael W. Lemberger

But we needed the scissors to operate on the crow. Sometimes you have to bend the rules.

When we got to my house, I stopped. "Here's the plan. You wait out here with the crow. I'll sneak into the house and get my mother's scissors. We'll operate on the crow in the backyard. O.K.?"

"Right," Royce whispered.

I heard my mother in the kitchen and slipped in the front door. I tiptoed through the house and into her sewing room. In front of me stood her beloved Singer sewing machine. On top of it rested her prized scissors. I snatched them up and started back out of the house. A survival instinct whispered to me that this might not be a good idea. I shrugged it off and eased out the front door.

There in the yard waited Midnight, Royce, and the crow.

"All right, hold on to the crow." I said and stepped forward, the open scissors poised in my hand.

Royce took a deep breath and clamped the crow to his chest. Midnight got up on his haunches, probably anxious to watch history being made. I steeled my resolve and stepped forward. Through some process of mental transference, the crow *knew* what I was going to do and wanted no part of it.

I jabbed at the crow and he ducked. I tried again and failed. That bird had more head fakes than Muhammad Ali. Then the crow cut loose with loud raucous calls of alarm. Royce bravely held on while the frantic crow gouged bloody furrows across his chest. Midnight started to howl. A neighbor lady hanging up clothes and watching the episode almost swallowed a clothespin. Then my mother appeared on the back porch.

"Tony! Royce! What are you boys doing?" she had to shout to be heard over the crow's pleas for help.

"Nothing," I answered. (That answer never did work.)

"What are you doing to that crow?"

"Nothing," I reassured her. (Just as well try it again.)

In an instant, she was in the yard next to us.

"Give me my scissors." Mom held out her hand.

"Mom, that crow's going to make us rich. What we need to do is—"

"What you need to do is give me my scissors."

I turned over my surgical instrument. Our chance to get rich was slipping away.

"Royce, let the crow go. Now."

Royce released the crow and it flew away, vowing revenge.

Mom took Royce in the house for repairs and soaked his bloody shirt in water. I was ordered to my room. It was going to be a long day.

THE CHICKEN THAT DIED THREE TIMES

Royce, Pat Donohoe, Bobby Howell, and I all had slingshots. We carried them in the back pockets of our jeans. For safety's sake, the rubbers were wrapped around the wooden fork. That kept them from being caught on something, stretched, and released, slapping us in our posteriors. The pouch of the instrument was a piece of leather usually cut from the tongue of my shoe. We got the rubber straps from ruined inner tubes we begged from oil stations.

At least once a day the four of us would walk south on Clinton Street and go under the railroad bridge. It was a quick slide down the grade to the tracks. On the railroad bed between the rails and ties lay thousands of pebbles, about the size of marbles. We'd fill both front pockets with shooter rocks.

But caution was the byword. Boys from the south side of the bridge also came to the tracks to replenish their ammunition supplies. Sometimes we would see them coming and hide in the weeds and sumac. If we had time, we would plan an ambush and catch them in a crossfire. But that ambush business cuts both ways. I'm here to tell you it's more fun to be the ambusher than the ambushee. Why no one ever lost an eye, I'll never know.

After one successful battle, we strutted north on South Clinton Street, bragging and looking for something else to shoot. Sparrows were high on our list and so were cats. Tin cans would do, or any unusual protuberance. Somehow, not everyone liked us.

Housewives stood on their porches with arm folded, and watched us saunter by. Empty glass milk bottles that sat on front steps were *verboten*; the same was true for white sheets that hung from clotheslines.

Between our destination and us was the house and chicken yard of Mister_____ whom we despised. We'd had trouble with him before. He had a garden down by the cemetery next to the tracks. The four of us were picking his blackberries one afternoon when he showed up in his Model A. He saw us and yelled. We ran across the tracks and hid behind a pile of logs. That old devil shot a .22 rifle over our heads five or six times. Those bullets hummed like bees. Then he fired some rounds into the logs just to show us he was serious. Afterwards we thought about telling our parents – there would have been holy hell to pay. On the other hand, we were picking and gobbling down *his* blackberries. Best to let the whole thing slide, we decided.

In perfect innocence and with no thoughts of revenge in mind, we strolled down the alley by his chicken yard. Mister_____ came out of the house and accused us of shooting his chickens. We didn't (honest) and told him so in clear terms he could understand. Mister_____ scorched us with some swear words I hadn't yet learned. We counterattacked, exhausted our vocabulary, and went on.

I came home at noon and knew I was in trouble. My father was waiting for me. It seems that Mister_____ went uptown to see him abut me shooting one of his chickens. Dad paid him a dollar for damages. I denied shooting a chicken or even shooting around this chicken yard. Alas, it was to no avail. Adults get believed before nine-year-old boys.

That night Dad came home in a twitter. He'd call Mister_____ a crooked S.O.B. and then laugh for a while. Finally, Mom got out of him what was wrong. Dad said he called the other two fathers and compared notes. It seems that Mister_____ accosted Patsy Donohoe about the dead chicken and got a dollar. Then he went to Bobby Howell's father and got a dollar from him. All for the same chicken!! After all these years, I look back on Mister_____ with mixed feelings. From early on I learned YOU DON'T CHEAT IN BUSINESS. But you have to give Mister_____ credit; he saw an opportunity and took it.

WINTER SPORTS BEFORE TV

Our slingshots were all put away for another season. Snowball fights were common, either on the way to school or going home. Our jeans would be frozen to our knees when we got into school. They would thaw, be wet and cold. Around mid-morning, they would dry out. I don't think anyone even caught a cold.

Rabbit hunting was great in the snow. You could track the furry little creatures and when you flushed one, wait. They always run in a circle. They hop around looking about and stop. Kerbam! Shoot them with your rifle.

One guy had a Beagle and I hunted with him a lot. I had a 20-gauge Iver Johnson single barrel and still use it ever so often. I made payments on a 20-gauge Stevens Pump that cost sixty-five dollars from the Western Auto Store. I was proud of that sucker and wish I had it back.

Ice-skating was a blast. We skated on the country club lake. The big games were hockey, tag, and crack-the-whip. If you were ever on the end of that line and the circle comes along, you can't hold on and you don't dare fall. Finally, the centrifugal force is too great. You have to let go. In order to keep from falling and plowing ice with your nose, you sort of hunch down and skate straight ahead, nothing fancy. Your eyes burn from the speed and after a hundred yards or so, you slow down enough to skate back to the crowd.

Royce, Sonny, and I both had short sleds. A short sled's easier to carry. We sledded at the golf course on the hill north of number six green. On a nice winter Sunday afternoon, there might be fifty people there. Someone would build a fire and we'd slide down the hill and walk back up. When it got too dark to sled safely, we'd all hike the necessary mile home.

But the best place to sled was the Loops. The Loops were south of the tracks and opposite of _____'s blackberry patch. The Loops are a series of three protuberances that jut out of the face of a long hill. These bulges are not an original part of the topography and might be Indian mounds for all I know. The third knob is a lulu. A sledder goes over that one like a miniature ski jump. You literally fly through the air and to the bottom of the hill at a terrific speed. A frozen creek with a steep bank lies at the bottom, and it's a good idea to bail out before you get there.

Yesterday Sonny Williams told me the flat ground below the Loops was called Death Valley. I'd forgotten that, but it sounds like a name we'd use.

The crème de la crème was a steep hill just west of the Loops that we called the Nutcracker. The Nutcracker was a long narrow hill that terminated in Death Valley. It had a six-foot spanned open crest that was bordered by trees and brush. In order to avoid getting ripped up by the brush or becoming part of a tree, one had to keep his sled in the spine-like opening. But the clear ground was deceptive. The Nutcracker bore the crenelations of a giant washboard under the snow. At the bottom was a two-foot lump your sled had to go over. The trouble was, the steepness of the hill made jumping off a bad idea. You were in for a long ride regardless of the pain. A boy rode the Nutcracker once on his belly. After that, he rode her sitting down.

Whenever a new guy came out, we always told him to ride the Nutcracker on his belly. That's what real men do. Only sissies ride a sled sitting down.

Our victim would take a run and fling himself down in the snow. When his sled hit those bumps, his body would bounce on his sled like a dribbled basketball. We boys would grimace and shake our heads. At the end of his ride, the victim would lie on his sled and twitch for minute or two. With difficulty, he'd get up, his eyes glazed with pain. The poor guy would walk bull-legged towards us taking short, mincing steps. We would try to keep straight faces. Life can be cruel.

SOONER'S FUNERAL

Sooner was a beagle/rat terrier mix, as I recall. He was a loyal dog and a boy's true friend. He and his master, Sonny Williams, had an unbreakable bond. Sooner followed us on our daily fun, be it playing ball or stealing apples.

One day in the summer of '44, Sonny, Sooner and I were exploring. We followed the creek at the south end of Oak View Cemetery and came out on Highway 34 at the bottom of the hill below the present-day St. Mary's Church. Sooner crossed the highway behind us and got sandwiched between two passing cars. Good-bye, Sooner.

Sonny was disconsolate. I picked up the mortal remains of Sooner and we took turns carrying him to his master's house. I left Sonny there with his consoling mother and went to my own neighborhood. Royce and Pat Donohoe were playing outside, and I gave them the sad tidings.

That evening I got a phone call from my bereaved buddy telling me the funeral was in the morning at 9:00 in his back yard. Royce and Pat were invited, too. The next morning I stopped over for my pals. The three of us, dressed in suits and neckties, solemnly walked down the alley in a light drizzle to Sonny's house. I was nervous. At the age of nine, I was going to direct my first funeral.

The grave was neatly dug right east of their driveway. After motioning Royce and Pat to stand next to the dirt pile, I went into the open garage. Sooner's boxed remains lay in state inside the door. Royce and Pat stood still with bowed heads as I carried Sooner's cold body to the grave. Sonny followed behind me, walking in dignity.

I eased Sooner into the grave and gave the barest of nods to Pat. He must have almost memorized a eulogy to the dog and he spoke long and well. Not to be outdone, Royce talked next, praising Sooner for qualities no five dogs could possibly possess. I spoke last and mercifully, short. Together the four of us said a prayer for Sooner.

The service was over. We all shook hands with the bereaved and assured him Sooner was in Dog Heaven. Then we went into Sonny's house and had milk and cookies.

THE CHRISTMAS RIFLE

One summer day in 1947, Sonny Williams and I moseyed into the Western Auto Store to look at sporting goods. Sonny walked past the gun rack and froze. Above him and just out of reach was a Remington single-shot .22 rifle. Sonny was entranced. He asked to see the rifle and the storekeeper kindly handed it to him. The price for the piece was around ten dollars as memory serves. That was a lot of money for a twelve-year-old in 1947. They finally struck a deal, and Sonny agreed to make payments of fifty cents a week. On Christmas Eve, he paid off the rifle and proudly took it home.

Christmas afternoon Sonny called me. He couldn't contain himself and had to repeat his words three times. I had to come right over. It was a good afternoon to go hunting. I grabbed my .22 Marlin and after a hurried explanation to my exhausted parents, tore out the door.

I arrived at his house in minutes. Sonny met me on his back porch, rifle in hand. No twelve-year-old was ever any happier. An aura of confidence and pride of ownership surrounded him. Reverently my pal handed me THE RIFLE. The piece's beautifully blued metal parts lay nestled in a polished walnut stock. The chromed bolt assembly gleamed with all the elegance that helped make Remington famous. I compared it to my own Marlin and reassured myself that mine was better. Why, hadn't I slain hundreds of squirrels and rabbits already with my trusty Marlin? Well, *hundreds* might be a little high. But this was Sonny's moment, and I praised his rifle most eloquently. When I stopped for breath, my pal yelled through the house to his parents that we were going hunting, and we were out of there.

We cut south through a brushy pasture onto the railroad tracks and walked west with Oak View Cemetery lying to our north. A stretch of bottomland between the tracks and the cemetery always held rabbits—at least rabbit tracks. It was a mild winter afternoon, as I recall. A soft north wind teased the snow on our boots. A pallid sun squinted through a layer of gray clouds. The air smelled wet. It would snow before morning. Walking kept us warm. We wore old clothes and stocking caps, but scorned gloves or mittens. Both of us carried WWII gas mask packs that served as game bags.

"Hey, shoot your new gun," I said.

"Not yet. I have to have something to shoot at."

"Just look around," I explained. "There's fence posts, trees. Sparrows." My hand wave included most of the known world. "We could probably find a can if we looked very hard."

"No, the first shot has to mean something. It has to be important."

I shrugged. We walked along in a companionable silence for the next ten minutes. I noticed an abundance of likely targets but wisely said nothing. (I don't always do that.) I saw the rabbit first. Our quarry squatted at the edge of a clearing. Behind it, black tree limbs were silhouetted against the white snow. The rabbit sat sideways to us, ears slanted back and furred rump humped up.

"Look!" I pointed to the clearing and cocked my Marlin.

"Let me shoot first! It's my first shot with my new rifle!"

I wanted that shot—brand-new rifle or not. My mind seethed. I saw the rabbit first. I get first shot! That's the rules! But it was Sonny's big day.

The rabbit hopped about two feet and stopped, looking down at something.

"He'll get away!"

"All right. Go ahead, shoot," I said and shouldered my Marlin.

The shot was difficult. My pal was shooting from a standing position with open sights. The distance was fifty, sixty yards down hill in fading light. I remember thinking I could make that shot. Maybe. Maybe not. His Remington cracked in the winter air Headshot; the rabbit leaped high and fell dead on the snow.

"Got him!" Sonny shouted. "I got him!"

"If you hadn't of—I would have," I said rather weakly. "Nice shot!"

We collected the dead rabbit and started towards his house. I can't remember a happier, prouder boy. I learned one of life's rules that day. A rule I wished I had followed more often.

CHRISTMAS DAY 1942

Christmas day in 1942 was cheerless. The casualty reports grew longer by the day. The German general, Rommel, was racing across Africa; the Japanese tide in the Pacific seemed irresistible. Kids got wooden sleds for Christmas. One of my great-aunts made orange peel candy that even I couldn't eat. Four of my uncles were in uniform, three of them in combat zones. My uncle Dan, and my father were exempt: both had contracted tuberculosis from unpasteurized milk when they were boys.

We went to Mass Christmas morning, and Father Heinen spoke of the terrible war and the bravery of our pope. He told us that the pontiff's Christmas Eve message had been a scathing denunciation of the Nazi treatment of the Jews, and that Pope Pius XII had delivered his message while being in Rome surrounded by Nazis and Fascists.

After Mass, we filed out of the old Saint Mary's Church and stood in family clusters as Catholics always do, the December snow drifting down. Mrs._____ had written the Pope several years ago and got a perfunctory reply – from a staff secretary, I suppose. She went from group to group, the much-creased letter held high and said, "I gotta da letter from a da Pope! We're a gonna da win now!"

The parishioners hid smiles behind gloves and scarves and nodded politely Somehow, I knew at the age of seven that things were going to turn out all right.

NEW YORK TIMES EDITORIAL, Christmas Day, 1942

No Christmas season reaches a larger congregation than the message Pope Pius XII addresses to the war-torn world at this season. *This Christmas, more than ever, he is a lonely voice crying out in the silence of a continent.* The Pulpit whence he speaks is more than ever the Rock on which the Church was founded, a tiny island lashed and surrounded by a sea of war. In these circumstances, in any circumstances, indeed, *no one would expect the Pope to speak as a political leader, or a war leader, or in any other role than that of a preacher ordained to stand above the battle, tied impartially, as he says, to all people and willing to collaborate in any new order which will bring a just peace.*

But just because the Pope speaks to and in some sense for all the peoples at war, the clear stand he takes on the fundamental issues of the conflict has greater weight and authority. When a leader bound impartially to both sides condemns as heresy the new form of national state which subordinates everything to itself; when he declares that whoever wants peace must protect against "arbitrary attacks" the juridical safety of individuals; when he assails violent occupation of territory, the exile and persecution of human beings for no reason other that race or political opinion, when he says that people must fight for a just and decent peace in "total peace" –the impartial judgment is like a verdict in a high curt of justice.

Pope Pius expresses as passionately as any leader on our side of the war aims of the struggle for freedom when he says that those who aim at building a new world must fight for free choice of government and religious order. They must refuse that the state should make of individuals a herd of whom the state disposes as if they were a lifeless thing.

After the war Pope Pius XII was hailed as "the inspired moral prophet of victory" and "enjoyed near-universal acclaim for aiding European Jews." Numerous Jewish leaders including Albert Einstein, Israeli Prime Minister Golda Meir, and Moshe Sharett praised him as a "righteous gentile." Israeli historian Pinchas Lopide concluded Pius XII saved at least 700,000 but probably 860,000 Jews from certain death at the "Nazi hands."

THE RELUCTANT CANDLE

Like all the other Catholic boys that grew up in Albia in the 1940s and 50s, I was an altar boy from age six to eighteen. Our priest was a strict old school German. He was a strong man, iron-willed, and honed by years of adversity from the Ku Klux Klan. A drill sergeant never ran a platoon more strictly than our priest ran the Sacristy. Looking back, he had to do it that way. To call us boys high-spirited would be an understatement.

Before Sunday Mass, twelve candles had to be lit. This wasn't Church doctrine, I'm sure. We just did it that way at Saint Mary's. Two altar boys were sent out to light six candles. Sounds simple, right? Three candles on either side of the tabernacle were easy enough to reach. But the other six were on the back of the altar and *waaay* up there. One candle would never light. Father with his Teutonic direct thinking would not brook any deviation. No obstacle will stop us. The candles will all be lit.

You don't know what lonely is until you are up there trying to light that one recalcitrant candle. Your body is stretched to its utmost, arms locked and above your head. Your ex-buddy, the one that helped light the other candles, has deserted you. The Sacristy is silent, the air tense. The priest gives a hiss that, in this case means, *Get it done quickly!* Behind you, the church is silent; two hundred pairs of eyes are watching you. You can feel your mother praying. You wish with every ounce of your being that you were somewhere else. Anywhere—even school!

The flame from the candle lighter is unseeingly probing for the candlewick. You try tiny circular motions hoping to find the wick and ignite it. A tendril of white smoke drifts upward. Aha! Success! No, the flame on your candle lighter went out. You lower the lighter, which you have come to hate, and slide the keeper upwards. This makes the wick about three inches long. After touching the wick to a lit candle, you have a miniature fireball. If hisses could echo, the ones emitting from the Sacristy would. With arms fully extended, you settle this conflagration down on the candle top.

There is a certain gathering, almost an audible sigh of relief from the congregation. Without looking, you *know* the candle is burning. You lower the candle lighter, whose flame has grown to blowtorch proportions, and snuff it out. A hasty genuflect, and you hurry to the Sacristy. The priest gives you a curt nod of approval. You join the queue of black-robed altar boys and follow the procession out to the altar.

Old St. Mary's
Church, Albia

BY HELL, FATHER, I FORGOT 'EM!!

In 1943, the war was grinding into its second full year. The people at home, already exhausted from the Depression, still went about their business with a quiet optimism. But there wasn't much to laugh about. Local men were being killed and wounded every week. Our priest would announce the latest casualties from the altar at Sunday Mass. Gold star flags hung from windows all over the county.

Things were tough by today's standards. Treadle Singer sewing machines hummed as housewives made clothes from chicken feed sacks. Every yard in Albia boasted fruit trees and vegetable gardens. Most folks kept chickens or rabbits. Squirrels were nonexistent in town. Gas was rationed; we had ration books for groceries and shoes.

At Saint Mary's Catholic Church, parish life conformed to the new reality. We had two Masses in those days, one at 8:00 for the city people and the second for country people at 9:30. A group of Irish nuns at Georgetown (eight miles away) came in after last Mass every Sunday to teach the children Catechism. A weekly roster was kept and every Sunday a different adult male was posted to get the sisters. That meant that the driver selected had to go to first Mass, drive to Georgetown and bring the sisters back to Albia by the time the 9:30 Mass was over.

People were more pious in those days. Church was well attended. We got there on time and didn't leave early. A worshiper came in the church, blessed himself, and found an empty pew. Those that were physically able knelt down, looked straight ahead and said their prayers. No nonsense. There was a rule that was inviolate: no one talked or giggled in church.

I was an eight-year old altar boy at the time, and I can attest to the truthfulness of what happened on that fateful Sunday at 9:30 Mass. Our priest had started his sermon. I scooted back on my stool and had just shifted my mind into neutral when I heard these words:

"Patrick, weren't you supposed to get the sisters today?" Father's booming voice would have been the envy of a Marine Corps drill sergeant.

A man in the middle of the crowded church jumped up. His snapped fingers sounded like a rifle shot. "By hell, Father, I forgot 'em!"

"Sit down, you fool!" the priest roared.

A titter of suppressed laughter rippled through several rows of worshipers. The priest grimaced, and bit his lip. His shoulders shook. He looked at the ceiling as if seeking guidance or forgiveness and started to laugh. The whole church rocked with laughter, a completely unrestrained mirth that echoed off the walls and went on for minutes. Finally, Father wiped his eyes and signaled for silence.

"There will be no sermon today and no catechism," he said. He turned, and started the second part of the Mass.

COUSIN DANNY, UNCLE DICK, AND THE BEAST

In 1947, the war had been over for two years and the economy was getting back to normal. There was a huge demand for new cars, and the funeral home bought a new De Soto to use as an ambulance. This purchase retired what we all called The Beast. The Beast was a '35 seven-passenger Plymouth that had been converted into an ambulance. It was an elegant machine with high arching front fenders and chromed headlights attached to them. As my grandfather used to say, "It is one hell of a mud car."

Uncle Dick acquired the Plymouth. He loved The Beast. He kept it parked on a half-circle drive under a catalpa tree between the funeral home and the alley. There it would sit in its majestic splendor, almost a relic, because in those days cars didn't last that long. Maintenance on The Beast was a chore, and woe be to the niece or nephew that strayed too close. They were put to work with wax can and soft rag caressing and buffing the Plymouth until it shined with celestial radiance.

One Sunday afternoon Cousin Danny and I were moseying down the alley when Uncle Dick spied us. We were immediately put to work waxing The Beast. We worked steadily in the summer sun hurrying to get the job done. Uncle Dick would come out of the house from time to time and check our progress.

We got pretty well done except for the curved top and the roof. I held Danny up and he got most of it. The roof was out of our reach and since Danny didn't weigh much, I suggested that he climb on top of The Beast and polish the roof. Then we would be done and could go do something constructive. He agreed and I boosted him up. I did not know the Plymouth had a cardboard top. Anyhow, Danny got up on the roof about the same time Uncle Dick came outside to inspect our work. Dick was standing on the porch, the screen door in his hand, as he yelled something harsh to Danny. Danny waved back and fell through the roof. He landed in the interior of the Plymouth on a welter of empty beer cans. Dick cut loose with a string of imaginative swear words that scorched paint off the funeral home wall and ran for his beloved car, murder in his eye.

He jerked open one side door while Danny squirted out the other. The footrace was on. They ran down the alley and crossed South Clinton Street heading west down another alley. I was convulsed in helpless laughter. Cousin Danny was putting them up and setting them down— Uncle Dick behind in hot pursuit running for revenge—Danny running for his life. Mortal fear adds impetus to one's running speed. Danny outdistanced him and hid in a copse of horseweeds that grew in most back alleys in those days.

Grandfather came out and asked me what had happened. Tears running down my face, I gasped and pointed to the ruined roof. Grandfather gave me a long look that said he knew I was somehow involved in this affair. He glanced at the holed roof, shook his head, and went back inside. I decided that a discreet withdrawal might be in my best interest.

THE CIVIL WAR MUSKET AND THE OUTHOUSE

I was at a fiftieth wedding anniversary where I ran into an old buddy, Larry Arnold, and his lovely wife, Ann. After handshaking and the obligatory, *"How's your family?" "Fine. How's yours?"* sort of thing, Larry reminded me of the time I shot the railroad's outhouse with a Civil War musket. We all have a self-protecting mechanism that allows us to remember some incidents and forget others. You might have heard that I've done some things that were plain dumb and others that fall in the category of monumentally stupid. This was one of those.

Larry, several others of our chums, and I was out hunting. I carried an 1823 U.S. Springfield .69 caliber musket that day. My resources were running a tad low, so I bought some black powder, shot, and a dozen percussion caps. We walked east on the railroad tracks ostensibly looking for rabbits and chewing Redman tobacco. We'd talk and spit, turning perfectly white snow into an ugly brown.

The rabbits weren't cooperating and we got bored. The conversation turned to girls, whom we didn't understand, to teachers whom we despised, and finally to who had the best gun. That led to a rather spirited discussion. We rounded a curve in the tracks and ahead of us, on the right of way and perhaps a hundred yards distant, stood an outhouse. You know, a privy.

One of the boys said, "I bet you can't hit that outhouse from here with that old gun."

"I could if I wanted to, but muskets are a close-range gun," I answered. "I intend to use shot in my musket to shoot rabbits. That requires the use of bird shot. Hitting a target like that outhouse would require a musket ball." (When you are thirteen, you are an expert on most everything.)

"Oh sure, well, let's see a musket ball," someone sneered.

I dug in my pocket and produced a round lump of lead about the size of a large marble that weighed around two ounces. I held the chunk of lead shoulder high between my index finger and my thumb. Waved it in a half circle for all to see. "This is a musket ball."

"You can't hit that privy from here. You're too chicken to try it," a detractor said.

"Well, it's a long shot," I said trying to cover myself. "What if someone's in it?"

"Ain't nobody in that old thing. It probably belongs to the railroad. They have them around for men on the extra gangs," somebody volunteered.

"Shoot it."

"You chicken?"

I loaded that old relic with a double charge of black powder and using the original ramrod, tamped down some newspaper for wadding. Trying to act confident, I slid in the musket ball and snuggled it on top of the paper. I elevated the barrel to a forty-five-degree angle and squeezed one off. The Springfield bucked and roared with an explosion that echoed and re-echoed throughout those frozen hills. The musket spit out a noxious cloud of stinking black powder smoke. My ears rang and my shoulder became a living agony. I knelt below the acrid fumes and watched a board flop loose on the grievously wounded privy.

We hurried to my target. I tried to act nonchalant, as if this shot was an everyday occurrence. On the snow, we saw where the impact of the slug had rocked the wooden structure. The lead slug made an entrance hole maybe the size of a quarter and on the opposite wall, an exit hole two inches in diameter.

The boys looked at me with a new respect. I accepted their praise, nodded, and knew in my heart of hearts I had just made the luckiest shot in Monroe County and perhaps the whole state. Lucky? I was lucky to be alive. A double charge of black powder in a one hundred and fifty year old gun is a recipe for suicide. I should have been super-dead and the gun ruined. With feigned nonchalance, I reloaded my musket with shot and spat tobacco juice on a railroad tie.

"Let's go rabbit hunting," I said.

I gave the musket to one of my nephews when he graduated from West Point. It's

probably sitting on a wall in his office somewhere. I *know* he's got enough brains not to shoot it.

THE GOLF BUSINESS

In the summer of 1945, four of us boys decided to become caddies. The going rate for carrying clubs nine holes and watching where errant golf balls went was fifty cents. That wasn't bad money when you consider a Coke sold for a nickel. Carts were unheard of. Everybody walked. Show up in the now-fashionable shorts, and you would have been laughed off the course.

I became the regular caddy for Mister Smith who ran the Smith Drug store on the west side of the square. He played in a group that included himself, Doctor Hannum, Doctor Scott, and Mark Pabst. These honorable men were thorough gentlemen. I could have learned a lot from them if I had stayed around. The other caddies of the group were Sonny Williams, Tom Roan, and Royce Donohoe. Billy Feehan, the Miletich brothers, Jerry and Jack, also caddied, but it must have been for another foursome.

Those men hit the ball well with those wooden-shafted clubs. For instance, when they teed off going to number three, we caddies waited north of the second hill by a large oak tree, which is still there, I think. The golfer's shot would land somewhere on the face of the second hill. That's about what most golfers' drives travel today with their graphite clubs. Going to eight, they always hit over the road and up on the fairway in good shape. Golf scores were some pars, lots of bogies, and a few double-bogies.

About halfway up the eighth fairway stood an old hand pump. Everybody always stopped for a drink of water. Mister Smith carried a tin cup on his golf bag. I always thought that was neat, a man thinking ahead like that. Three apple trees grew in the vicinity of the pump. Nothing quite like green apples and cold water on a hot summer day!

I found an easier way to make money and quit the caddying business cold. Why walk around those hills carrying someone else's golf bag when you could go out in the cool of the morning and make two, maybe three dollars? Golf balls were scarce after the war and money was still tight. We walked the edge of the course and looked for lost balls. A twelve-year-old boy who knows the things money can buy has the vision of an eagle. We soon learned to look for a round edge of white, not the whole ball.

The lake was a prime place to find balls. Sixty years ago, before the west end of the lake was filled with silt, there was a footbridge across the lake going to number five green. The water under the bridge was maybe five or six feet deep in the middle. The lake was clear and you could see clams on the bottom. There was always a wooden homemade jon-boat lying unattended on the south bank next to a dock. We would bail it out and using boards for oars, paddle over to the bridge. A white golf ball really looms up from the bottom of the lake, and after a weekend of a tournament play, we might get twenty or thirty balls.

We got sharp real quick. A Titleist golf ball was the top of the line and worth more money. Wilsons were all right, the others just so-so.

The golfers hit the links in the middle of the afternoon. Around three o'clock, they would start to show up in the parking lot. Sonny and I, loaded down with our wares, would smile and drift over to the locker room door. We'd wait for them to come out, hearing laughter inside, locker doors slamming, and steel cleats grinding on concrete. The opportune time to approach a customer was when they stepped outside, bag in hand. Many a sale was made on that strip of sidewalk just west of the locker room door.

The price of a used golf ball was determined by its bounce. The seller held the ball to his forehead and dropped it on concrete. If it bounced to his knees, it was worth a nickel. A bounce as high as his belt fetched a dime. A bounce to his chest meant a good ball and was worth fifteen cents. A pristine Titleist golf ball was open for negotiations and might bring from a quarter up.

But times change. Hardly anyone walks the course anymore. Grown men, including myself, wear walking shorts and ride in golf carts. The apple trees and the pump are gone along with my boyhood.

CHEWING TOBACCO AND TERRORIZING BUCK

About the time I was a freshman in high school, we discovered chewing tobacco. Plug tobacco was strong stuff but it looked cool in one's shirt pocket if his parents were out of sight. It was impressive, we thought, to fish out a plug and bite a chew off it in front of some girls. These young ladies were not too impressed, as I recall. It wouldn't have mattered. We were afraid to ask them out anyway .We eventually went to something milder and bought Redman or Beechnut. I could handle that.

My chewing buddies included Royce Donohoe, Bill Feehan, and Jay Sullivan. Summer nights the four of us would sit on the courthouse steps. We would chew, spit on the grass, and talk about most anything. Eventually we would get bored and go look at the television set a merchant had in his store window. It had a real snowy picture and most folks thought TV would never amount to much.

It doesn't take much to bore young men, especially when it's too early to go home and too late to start a new project. One of us spied our good buddy, Buck, with a step ladder outside the King Theater. Buck's job was to put up a new sign on the marquee that announced the change in movies. He would climb a shaky stepladder and take down the old letters. Then he would arrange the new letters in the proper sequence and with them tucked under his arm, climb the ladder and install them on the marquee. Scaring Buck was great sport, but he was wise to us – so it required great cunning and stealth.

We ran north past the Light and Railway building and cut east down the first alley. At the intersection of the alleys, we turned south and came out on Benton Avenue right next to the King Theater. I peeked around the wall and saw Buck in rapt concentration. He was perched on top of the ladder, straining to put a letter on the sign. At my silent signal, we all ran out on the sidewalk below Buck screaming like raiding Comanches.

Buck naturally shrieked in terror and grabbed for anything solid. The metallic letters and the stepladder came crashing down on the sidewalk. Our buddy Buck dangled in air clutching the marquee with a white-knuckled grip of fear. We were convulsed in laughter, holding our sides and almost falling down. After Buck pleaded long enough, somebody would set up the ladder. He would climb down to the sidewalk, his nerves destroyed. One of us would offer him a chew.

After his confidence was restored, Buck would sort out the scattered letters. We would promise not to scare him again (that night) and even help with the new sign. The plan was for Buck to get up on the ladder and we would hand letters up to him to place on the marquee. The new movie title was to be, say, "Six-Gun Law" starring Roy Rogers and Dale Evans. Somehow, the letters we handed up to Buck would get mixed up and "Six-Gun Law" would become -- well, you get the idea.

Buck would get through and climb down. He'd go out on the sidewalk away from the marquee to admire his work and see something awful up there. The four of us would break up in hysterics. When we recovered, Buck would still be gazing at the marquee as if contemplating the basic unfairness of life. Conscience-stricken, we jumped in to help our buddy and soon had the sign righted. By this time, it was nine o'clock and time to go home. Royce and I were neighbors. We walked home together, moseying down the elm-shrouded South Clinton Street, and secure in the knowledge we had done some good for the day.

SKINNY-DIPPING IN CEDAR CREEK

In the summer of 1947, Royce Donohue and I, together with a loose amalgam of three or four of our chums, decided to swim in Cedar Creek. Never mind the fact that our parents paid dues at the local country club so we could enjoy safe swimming. We hiked out on the Ward Road, which is an extension of Benton Avenue West, to the twin bridges, a distance of about four miles. The earlier high waters of the summer had left a magnificent swimming hole under the two bridges and right beside the road. The stream was unsullied in those days – no chemical run-off. It was a great place to swim, complete with a sandy bottom and deep clear water.

The east bank of the creek was the road, screened from the stream by a hodge-podge of willow saplings. A careful driver would come to the blind sharp turn of the road, stop and sound his horn several times before proceeding. He was often greeted with a flash of bare skin from behind the willows.

Two railroad bridges spanned the stream. Once, on a dare, we boys gingerly weaved through the brush and got up to the tracks. Our plan was to jump off the bridge into the creek. The rocks were hot on our bare feet and you soon learned to step on the ties. We no more got out on the trestle and a car came by. Modesty demanded that we crouch down on the tracks. Modesty? Hey, you can't skinny-dip with clothes on.

Anyway, there we were standing out in the middle of the trestle wearing our birthday suits and looking down at 'ol Cedar Creek. The subject soon came up as to who was going to jump first. Nobody really wanted to. In fact, you couldn't have pushed us off that bridge with a Mack truck. But twelve-year-old boys have to save face. The disjointed, faltering conversation went something like, "I'll go, if you go first." Followed by "Oh, no. I'll go, if *you* go first."

Royce stood next to me. I glanced at him and he shook his head slightly. He needn't have bothered. With the summer breeze whistling through my nether regions and Cedar

Creek looking like a skinny ribbon way, *way* down there, I *knew* I wasn't going to jump first – or last for that matter. We had just about mutually agreed that jumping was a bad idea -- of course, we were all too smart for that -- when a car came by and honked. We all crouched down. Too late. We'd been spotted. Now we can't jump! Someone might tell our parents! Almost cheering, we raced off that trestle, tore bare-skinned through the brush, which had somehow developed thorns, and into the sanctuary of Cedar Creek.

A new guy, who wanted to join our little clique, brought a kettle, butter, and salt and pepper. Before our daily swim, we invaded a nearby cornfield and must have stolen two bushels of immature field corn. We built a fire on a sandbar, filled the kettle with creek water, and threw in the shucked corn. There is no feeling like being twelve, sitting in the summer sunlight, and gorging yourself on stolen corn. A week later, high water struck again. It took away our kettle and left our swimming hole full of mud.

I heard that one guy with a death wish did actually leap into the creek from the bridge. He's still around, and to my knowledge, has led a perfectly sane life since his big jump.

FISHING

As boys, we fished in most every pond and lake in the county. Most of the time, we didn't have much luck. The only bright spot was Cottonwood Lake. Man, did we catch bullheads. We laced those pits with trot lines and fished all night. Away from parental supervision, we could smoke and cuss all we wanted.

We all owned bait-casting outfits with heavy lines and reels that backlashed continually. Sometimes we would save enough money to buy a fishing lure—maybe a hula-popper or a jitterbug. All they caught was moss. My Uncle Jim gave me a Shakespeare bamboo fly rod and some flies. I had an old boat at the country club and did well on the bluegills and crappies. When I went to the army, I stored my fly rod in the attic of the garage behind the funeral home. Two years later, it was gone. Welcome home, Soldier. Years later I saw the reel in the basement of a friend. Ah, well. Let it go.

Now I'm going to tell you how to catch fish in a Southern Iowa farm pond or even a lake. Buy a light-action six-foot spinning rod and an open-faced spinning reel. Order it out of Cabela's. They are not that expensive. Try to order the reel already loaded with four-pound test monofilament line. A line of that thin a diameter will not impede the action of the lure and will sink slowly. That is what you want. Buy *black* 1/64 ounce jigs, called "Little Nippers." They are made by Lindy. Bait the jig with a mealworm and cast it out next to a bed of moss. Retrieve in a slow pumping motion. It works wonders on any fish, especially big bluegills.

© Michael W. Lemberger

Most fish *rise* to feed. They wait for small insects to fall into the water. The motion of a small black jig drifting down the water column attracts them. The 'gill thinks "Aha! Food!" He swims towards it. The 'gill picks up the scent of the mealworm. The dinner bell is ringing. The 'gill will hurry towards the bait before another fish beats him to it. The 'gill mouths the bait and swims off. Set the hook and the rest is history.

Get bored catching bluegills? Use the same rig and six-pound test line if you have it. Tie on a 1/32-ounce black Little Nipper. Hook a six-inch nightcrawler through the nose and cast out to the edge of the moss. Keep your lure out of the green stuff. Let the worm fall for the count of three and retrieve it in a slow pumping motion. A bass or a channel cat will hit that bait like a freight train. Fight the fish holding the tip of your rod high. When hooked, a bass will instinctively go for the moss and break off. A cat will fight in open water. They fight sullenly and without the slashing run of a bass.

If you want to catch crappies, tie on a 1/64-ounce white jig and a white Mister Twister.

That's all the equipment you need to catch fish around here. Try it. If it doesn't work, don't tell me about it.

SQUIRREL HUNTING

Like every other fifteen-year old boy, I went out for football. Unlike every other fifteen-year old, I quit on the opening day of squirrel hunting season, September 15th. After a couple years of this, our coach lost interest in me. I liked the game, the guys, etc. The only thing was, I liked hunting better. Besides, I was expected to work at the store or the funeral home after school.

One summer in about 1950, my father presented me with a Marlin .22 rifle. It was a bolt action with a tubular magazine and a peep sight. He obtained the rifle by buying a certain quantity of embalming fluid. It was the best rifle I ever owned. I shot targets with it at measured distances and got proficient. Dad told me to buy .22 standard-velocity Remington shells and try them. Boy, they worked, too. My groups tightened right up.

When school started, my routine changed. If I was needed to work after school, somebody called the principal's office and I missed football practice. After hunting season started, it was good-bye football. After school, it was either work or hunting. During my junior year, I stuck with football and really got into it. Missed hunting like crazy. Grandfather told me, "Quit football." He worried if I got hurt, I couldn't work. I argued, and he played his trump card. Said if I was hurt too bad to work, I would surely be hurt too bad to hunt. I couldn't see myself limping around the woods with my foot in a cast. I quit football.

So, I went back to my routine of school, working, and/or squirrel hunting. I developed this method of hunting over time. I entered a shallow creek about a hundred yards from where I wanted to hunt. This kept down the noise of crashing through a leaf-carpeted stand of trees. I walked either in the shallow water or on the sand and stayed in the shadows. The squirrels never knew I was there.

Overhead tree limbs were laced together above the creek, and squirrels used them as a bridge. I walked slow and stepped easy. When a squirrel appeared, I shot him only if I could get a head shot. I marked the dead squirrel and let him lie. Usually I would get two on the creek.

After a half an hour or so of the creek walking, I'd go up a hillside and wait in the shadows of a long-gone white oak. I never shot the first squirrel that appeared. He was a decoy. I'd wait until there were three or four playing around and shoot one. He'd fall and I'd mark him. The crack of a .22 didn't seem to scare them. The survivors would freeze against a limb for a minute or so and continue to feed. I'd wait a few minutes and shoot another. Four was my self-imposed limit I would collect my game and start towards home.

I'd walk down the street on the way to the funeral home. Being young and proud of my skill, I carried my rifle slung over my shoulder and the squirrels in my hand so all could see. Sometimes I met a pretty girl from my class. I'd show her the slain squirrels. We'd chat a short time while she kept her eyes averted. (Girls don't like to look at fresh, head-shot squirrels.) Soon we would run out of words and I would go on, feeling that somehow things had gone sour.

Another block north and I'd cut down the alley by Shehan's. Alex Shehan (the Archibald brothers' grandfather) always seemed to be in his yard, and we would stop and chat. I'd brag about my squirrels. You know, four squirrels, four shots, etc. He would admire the game, and I'd offer them to him. Then his wife would call my mother and tell her I'd be late. Alex and I would sit and skin squirrels. I'm sure that relieved my long-suffering mother who cooked a lot of game for me.

Somebody got away with my Marlin and I'd give a lot to have it back. I'd give a lot more to go hunting with that 14-year-old boy again, the one who knew every game track in the creek bank. His enthusiasm was unbridled. He loved the busy hum of the insects, the cries of the birds, and the hammering sound of a woodpecker on a tree limb. He respected the animals he killed, always skinned them, and gave away as much game as he kept. It's hard to say where or when he left, but I sure wish he'd come back.

EXPELLED AND SAVED BY UNCLE DICK

Part way through my junior year in high school, things were going smoothly for me. I ate like a horse and worked in the store after school and Saturdays. When I wasn't working, I was running the woods, shooting small game and bringing it home for my sainted mother to cook. I had survived algebra and geometry with passing grades and got into studies that I some interest in such as history, Latin, and literature. At this period in my life, I wrote some poems. Mercifully, none of my efforts have survived the years.

My parents were more or less pleased with me. The discipline problem of my earlier years had disappeared. I still chewed tobacco but was smart enough not to get caught. Life was good. But even the best-behaved people can get into trouble.

It all happened in third-period study hall. I went back to the corner of the room to sharpen my pencil, and nodded at my classmate, Jerry K., who was going to his desk carrying a heavy dictionary. Jerry responded to my salutations by slamming me over the head with the dictionary. I punched him five or six times and pretty well had things under control when the teacher separated us. We were sent to the dreaded office to face the principal.

We were both given a chance to explain our positions. I possibly could have avoided trouble but I was pretty well steamed. I hadn't been kicked out of class all year, and here it was October. By my standards, that was outstanding behavior. My grades were reasonably good. This idiot had started the fight, not me. What was I supposed to do when someone, out of the blue, slugs me with a dictionary?

We both got expelled for three days. That meant no school Wednesday, Thursday, and Friday. But when you return to school, you must have a statement signed by your father stating that he is aware of your expulsion and your behavior will improve.

If my folks got word of my expulsion, I'd be dead. It would be all over. Good-bye, cruel world. I had to figure out a way to keep my parents from knowing what had happened. I had to run a con.

Missing school was no problem, and showing up for work after 3:30 was routine and not liable to rouse suspicions. That's what I did for the rest of the week.

Only one hitch. I had to have my father's signature and written acknowledgment of my expulsion. Forging wouldn't work; Dwight Humeston's signature was on record in the principal's office. It had been required to get me out of school on work permits. I agonized all weekend. Maybe I should just tell my folks. You know, just 'fess up.

I decided to run it past my Uncle Dick. I told him the whole situation. Everything. Dick said his signature was just like Dwight's. No one could tell them apart. Dick wrote me out a nice one-page letter and signed it. Monday morning I delivered it to the principal's office in fear and trembling. He read it, compared signatures and nodded.

"I expect that after what your parents said to you, you're going to behave yourself. Right?" He almost crowed.

"Right," I answered and went off to class.

BEER AND QUAIL DON'T MIX

One wintry November afternoon, I was walking down the railroad tracks just south of Oak View Cemetery hunting rabbits. I watched a car roll down one of those narrow cemetery roads and park. A high school chum of mine got out of the car and looked around very carefully. How he missed seeing me, I'll never know. After a short wait, he reached in the back seat and pulled out two large grocery sacks. He carried them into the graveyard and hid them behind a large gray tombstone. Again, he scanned the area, got in his car and left.

I walked on and shot some game in the woods that used to stand south of Saint Mary's new church. The mystery of the two sacks nagged at my mind all the time I was hunting. On the way home, I cut through the cemetery and walked close to the place where my buddy had secreted the two sacks.

I found the right tombstone without any difficulty. The two sacks each contained eighteen loose cans of beer. Aha! Should I take the beer? This posed a moral question. My school chum was sixteen, the same age as me. He had illegal beer! That's breaking the law! I have to protect him.... are we not our brother's keeper? Clearly, it's my Christian duty to keep my pal from getting into trouble.

With my conscience mollified, it was time to act. I slung my rifle and tucked a sack of beer under each arm. Loaded down with beer and rifle, I hiked to the west end of the cemetery, and hid the beer behind another tombstone. One of my buddies had a car, and there was a lane a short distance away. Under the cover of darkness, we could drive down there, park, take a short walk, and get the beer. It was a foolproof plan. Right? Right.

That night, four of us rode down the lane in our pal's old Chevy. We stopped at the place I had marked with my white handkerchief. I had hid the beer behind a tombstone thirty paces straight east. It was time to go into the cemetery and get the beer. I was ready to go but wanted someone with me. Two of the guys flatly refused to go. It was *spooky.*

My dad was an undertaker. I grew up in a funeral home, but I was still about half-freaked out. The wind had come up from the south and moaned through the trees. Gray clouds scudded across a restless sky and dimmed a quarter moon. The tombstones ahead of us looked like gray specters. Who knows what could be waiting in those trees?

Finally a kid we'll call Frank agreed to go with me. We had to walk through a strip of brush maybe ten feet wide to get to the cemetery. Got past it and out into the mowed grass. We both felt guilty about stealing the beer and a little afraid. I walked east and counted steps, staying between the rows of stones. I got confused. Frank kept falling behind me and I heard a part chant, part moan. Somehow, I kept my composure and asked Frank if he was making that noise. He said yes and that he was really, really scared. I called him a chicken and told him to come on. I walked a little deeper into the cemetery and heard a car door slam. My ex-buddy Frank had deserted me.

I scraped up enough resolve to keep on going, and I found the beer. With a sack full of loose beer cans under each arm, I started back to the car. Usually fear is not one of my vices, but I felt a certain chill. I wanted to look behind me, but I knew that was silly.

After an eternity of walking, I saw the shine of the car's hood way to my right. Realizing I had somehow got confused in the cemetery, I started towards the road. A strange noise behind me caused me to shift gears from a fast walk into a hard run. I hit that strip of trees and stepped right into a covey of quail. My yell was proof positive that shrieks of terror can't wake the dead. The next afternoon we went back and found about half the beer.

FIGHTING

In the forties and the fifties, fist fighting was the accepted way to settle arguments between us boys. This developed into a pecking order, and you knew whom you could whip and whom you couldn't. Occasionally someone would try to elevate himself a notch or two, and the results, while sometimes successful, were always painful. Fights in the courtyard were a source of entertainment, and the unbloodied and unbruised onlookers cheered the pugilists on. The City Police, after watching for a while, would break them up and send everybody home. That was hometown Monroe County Justice.

I saw high school football games stopped because people ran across the field to watch a fist fight. The police would wade through the spectators and separate the combatants. If the belligerents were local boys, they were admonished and advised to go home. If one of the fighters was an out-of-towner, he could expect to go to jail and be fined for disturbing the peace.

I did not witness the following incident but I heard about it from the battlers.

One summer day in say, 1953, a road crew was repairing a street in front of a local Albia tavern. The front door of the tavern was open and young men inside were basking in the fans and drinking cold beer. Outside, in the hot sun, other young men were sweating on the bricks and pouring asphalt. It started as teasing, with the drinkers heckling the workers and waving beaded mugs of beer in their direction. Soon insults were exchanged. Challenges to individual combat were issued and accepted.

Without warning, there was an eruption. The workers had had enough. They threw down their tools and charged the tavern. The drinkers gleefully met them in battle. The fight flowed out of the tavern and onto the sidewalk. The combatants rolled in the freshly tarred street. The police that came to break up the donnybrook could hardly keep from laughing. Not wanting to get sticky with tar themselves, they stood on the sidewalks, shouted and blew whistles. The fight ended as quickly as it started. The drinkers went in search of kerosene to clean their clothes, and the laborers returned to their work.

No fines were levied, no charges were filed. Monroe County Justice circa the 1950's.

One summer night when I was home from college, a carnival came to town. Royce and I were both about twenty-one – maybe twenty-two – and drinking beer with our buddies in a local watering hole. A bunch of carnies came in and a fistfight broke out. *Now, this is the truth, so help me. Royce and I decided to avoid trouble and go home!* Pretty good, huh?

We had started around the front of the hotel to get to my truck when five carnies jumped us. Now there are four rules in street fighting with strangers: One, chicken out, back down, whatever you want to call it. Two, walk away. Three, run away. Four, win. Our first three options were off the table, so we went for number four.

The battle raged between parked cars and a hedge that used to grow next to the sidewalk. When the police finally came, two of the carnies lay on the sidewalk. The carnies all got fined ten dollars each for disturbing the peace. I had a torn shirt and Royce a scraped elbow .The next night we all drank beer together. You figure it out.

In August of 1958, shortly before I went to the Army, I was at loose ends and soothing my nerves at a local pub when an argument broke out among the drinkers over who was the fastest runner. The debate grew heated and bets were made. Perhaps a dozen of us, both bettors and runners, all went out into the hot sunlight. The course was laid out—from the intersection of A Avenue West and North Clinton, south to the intersection of Clinton and Benton, (the northwest corner of the square) and back again.

This was in the middle of the afternoon during the week!

Maybe one hundred spectators lined the street to watch. When the foot race was over, the man I bet on won. I got paid, but some of the other bettors had a problem. A fight broke out and a welsher got a bloody face. He went to the law to press charges. He was ignored and told to go pay his bet.

That's the way things were around here fifty years ago.

THE SKUNK AND THE HOLEY BARN

This is a true story. I was there. For reasons that will soon become obvious, the names of the other two men have been changed to protect me from great bodily injury.

One fine summer day, _____ and I were fishing in Xxxx's farm pond when he shouted to us to come up to his barn. There was urgency in his voice. We ran like the dickens and got there all out of breath. Xxxx explained there was a skunk in his barn and he had been after it for a month. He had just seen it. Would we please kill it? He handed _____ an old hammer double barrel twelve.

"That's the least we can do for you," _____ said. "After all, you have let us fish here for years."

"I don't see any skunk. How do we go about flushing it out and shooting it?" I asked. The fish were biting, and I wanted to get back to the pond.

"Well," Xxxx said. "He stays behind those bales." Xxxx pointed to a space between the hay and the barn wall. "Tony, you climb up there with this pole and jab it down next to the wall where he lives. He'll come out in a hurry and then _____ can shoot him."

I had never heard of a skunk spraying upwards, so I agreed.

When I got on top of the bales, Xxxx said to _____, "Just cock one hammer at time. Those trigger springs are old and if both hammers are cocked, the shooting of one barrel sometimes sets the second off."

"Right," _____ said and looked determined.

I started at the edge of the bales, stabbing down to where Xxxx said the skunk was. A few minutes later, Monsieur Skunk came waddling out. He and _____ saw each other at the same moment. It was a scene out of a Western movie. The skunk wheeled to fire just as _____ cocked the shotgun hammers and raised the weapon to his shoulder. The skunk might have been a tad faster, because skunk juice travels slower that a shotgun charge. But they both hit their mark. The skunk was obliterated and part of him disappeared through an eight-inch gap in the barn wall. The recoil of the twelve gauge jerked the gun muzzle upright and the second barrel discharged making a jagged hole in the barn roof just above the eaves. I was out of danger of getting shot or gassed and collapsed on top of the hay in helpless laughter.

After composing myself, I went out the barn's back door and around to the front, being very careful to stay upwind. I peeked in the barn. _____ and Xxxx were standing in a fine mist as if trying to comprehend what had happened to them.

"Sometimes things don't quite work out as we planned," _____said.

Xxxx stopped coughing long enough to say," You got that right."

"Your shotgun sure made a hole in that wood," _____ said.

Xxxx squinted upwards at the brand-new skylight in his barn roof and said, "You got that right."

"Hey, old buddy—you want some fish? Tony and I'll even clean them for you." _____ was getting nervous.

Xxxx is a mountain of a man whose fists hang like hams. He turned his anger-flushed face to _____ in a series of jerks. "No, I don't want any @#!!(&%# fish!"

_____ practically ran to my truck and grabbed the door handle. I shook my head and pointed to the back end. He rode back there all the way home. I never did know what happened to the fish.

JAMSIE AND THE JAMES BOYS

Letters from Morrisons to my grandparents in Melrose
(Quoted in Father Leo Ward's book *Out of Nowhere*)
August 27 (1903)

Dear Children Joe and Maggie

Everyboddie has gone to the fair this week Nick Kearns and Frank Ohoro and frank and james Malone and Bush Ryan and pat Mullin and all the Massmans and ulums and Martins and Batties and Dave Shepard all drove in covered wagons.

Mollie and Nonie are getting the diner and it isn't like Joe's diner. It is potatoes and corn and corn and potatoes. Kittie is working on her rug and Jamsie is gone to the sale at Caddies. Conways had a dance o Monday Night. Mollie and Kittie were there.

I halve 3 gallon jar of cucumbers and a tub full and I can get a Bucket full every morning. I will give you all yu want.

From Mama or Mrs. James M.

I sepose yea will think I am getting sillie

October 24 (1903)

Dear children

I got year letter yesday and was glad yea were well I am feeling real well this week.

I maid a barrel of soap and a barrel of Crout this week and Notted a quilt and went to town and soad some on nell and Susie;'s Dresses all this week. Jimmie is husking corn and your paw is moving hay and wood all this week.

Martin knoles was married wensday and they just had a dinner and went to Chicago thursday. Frank ohoro is to be called tomorrow

Cassie wants you to see Mary and tell her to sind her Mary's last winter hat with you and save her of buying. johnies and Micks were all down last Sunday and stayed all day.

Johnie B's foot is all right. Jimmie put him down in the pasture and yea left and Kit

PHONE 51

BATES' CAFE

"WE EAT HERE OURSELVES"

MELROSE, IOWA   Sept. 20 '27

Dear Aunt Mary - I received your two letters, but I was too sick to answer the first one, but thank God I feel a little better now. I have been in bed nearly all summer and was very poorly. All the rest are well. Lois & everyone. The Wards are well. Jimmie & Gertrude came this way coming from the fair. They stayed one night at Dominic's & one at Martin's. Rosies are pretty well.

Maurice is in Des Moines at the Lutheran hospital. He didn't like Knox and came back. He is getting along very nicely.

Grandpa is well. He went to Ottumwa today for a new suit of clothes. Jimmie, Julia & Viola were in Nebraska & Sioux Falls. They just came back Friday. All are well, I guess.

Well Mary I am not able to write very much. Write again soon and pray for me to get well.

Good bye

Maggie

Miss Mary Morrison
Burlington,
Iowa

669 Iowa St.

drives may to school and what do you think but magie sulivan or Cor had twins tuesday night a boy and a girl and she was very bad she had to Docters and the priest. We are getting our carpet wove in Iconium. What was the trouble with Helen and Jennie that they didn't get a long. Richards is all well and mcgees are going to halve a dance Saturday night. Year little pigs are big ones now. Well I guess I cant think of any more to say so good by maggie and joe from

mama

My great-grandfather was James Morrison. He operated a survival farm several miles south of Melrose. He was widowed early in his marriage and raised eleven children, mostly girls. His admonition to his daughters when they went out at night was, "Whatever the weather, keep your legs together." Sometimes he would remember to add, "If you are out after midnight, you are not with the angels."

Anyhow, Jamsie, as most folks called him, was working on a rail fence when he saw a group of five horsemen on the main road. They exchanged waves and he watched them gallop towards him, their horses's bellies whopping on the prairie grass. The riders reined in close to him in a miasma of horse sweat and crushed grass. Up close, he saw they were tough-looking men, carrying rifles and sidearms.

The horsemen, through accident or design, hemmed him close to his fence. Now Jamsie was a successful brawler with honed survival instincts. While he was not scared, let's just say he was extremely alert. When one of the men asked directions to Walnut City, Jamsie told them in a polite voice.

There followed an uneasy silence. The men sat their horses, their bodies tense. A sorrel tossed his head and in a serpentine movement snatched a clump of grass by Jamsie's feet. Two of the men, who looked

40

James F. Morrison, holding a grandchild

enough alike to be brothers, exchanged glances and a silent message ran between them. Gremlins in Jamsie's stomach must have done acrobatics as he looked up at these stern-faced men on horseback.

"Do you know Jessie James?" one of the riders finally asked.

"No, sir, I don't. But I think he is a very fine man," Jamsie answered.

"Jessie James thinks you are a very fine man, too," the rider said.

The men rode away leaving Great-grandfather Morrison somewhat shaken, but alive.

EATING LIKE A KING IN MELROSE

Time was when at almost every Catholic funeral, the deceased was taken to the family's home for a wake. This caused the undertaker some extra work. My father and/or uncle would embalm and casket the body. The dearly departed would be placed in the hearse to take to the grieving family's house.

Royce and I would follow in a quarter-ton Ford truck. In the truck, we had a funeral tent, fifty folding chairs, kneeler, candles, and crucifix in suitcases and a velvet crepe badge for the front door. We would unload everything at the bereaved's house and then wheel up the hill to the cemetery and set up the tent. The men dug graves by hand in those days. In summertime, they needed shade. In wintertime, they needed a tent with a side curtain to cut the wind.

On the day of the funeral, Royce and I would arrive at the cemetery with greens, lowering device, planks and a wooden box for the casket. After the set-up was made, we drove to the house. The body and family were gone to the church by then. We picked up everything except the folding chairs. When that work was done, our job was to stay out of sight until the burial was over.

The neighbor ladies would be at the house cooking lunch, and my goodness, did they bring in food. They had fresh fruit pies, fried chicken, potatoes, scalloped corn, fresh green beans, ham, and all kinds of good chow for growing boys. Royce and I were sort of cons about it. We'd act shy and they would fuss over us. Royce would tell them his last name. Donohoe's Irish, of course. That helped. Most of the cooks went to school with my mother or knew my grandparents. I played that card for all it was worth. We'd hang around for a while and sure enough, they would ask us to eat. And did we! Feeding two fifteen-year old boys is like trying to fill up a stray dog. Gorged, we'd stagger out to the truck and go back to the cemetery. Over the years, I've dined in a number of fine restaurants. But some of the best meals I have ever eaten were in farm homes south of Melrose.

Ad for the Humeston Funeral Home, about 1927.

THE ESCAPING CORPSE

In the early days of the twentieth century, my grandfather, D. S. Humeston, was an undertaker in Albia. One brutal winter day he was called out to pick up a body northwest of Georgetown. The plan was for him to drive his hearse as far west as Fallon's Corner, which is a mile beyond Georgetown. Due to the high snow, a driver with a team and sledge would meet him there. He would take my grandfather, with a box for the corpse, north to the family's home. As was the custom, Grandfather would sell the casket by description and give the family a price. Then the men would load the corpse into the box and onto the sledge. The driver would deliver him back to his hearse at Highway 34.

Things went as planned. Condolences were offered, the corpse loaded and the three of them sleighed back through the deepening snow south towards Fallon's Corner. On the way, they picked up a man walking down the road. There was no room on the seat for the new passenger so; he clambered up on the box containing the corpse. Picture this: A well-muscled sorrel team trudging in deep snow with twin blasts of frozen breath steaming from their nostrils. They are pulling a wooden sledge. On the sledge are four riders; grandfather and the driver huddled deep in greatcoats, the corpse, and the new passenger perched high on the corpse's box.

When they approach the hearse, a crowd has gathered, standing respectfully with their heads bared. One wise guy breaks the solemnity and shouts, "Mister Humeston! Mister Humeston! Your corpse got out!"

EARLY DAYS

In the early days of the county, as far back as reliable records go, a fur trader named Eddy operated a trading post on the Des Moines River. He did business with a local thug named Chief Hardfish, and upon occasion, members of Kishkekosh's and Mahaska's tribes. Eddy would have received his trading goods by canoe coming up river and sent furs to civilization the same way. A major Indian trail ran south from Eddy's Post and after crossing the Des Moines River, followed the general route of Highway 137 to another Indian camp which is now the site of Albia.

In 1832, the U.S. Army defeated the Sauk, Fox, and Winnebago tribes in the Black Hawk Indian War. They captured Chief Black Hawk and made him an offer he couldn't refuse. The United States Government purchased a strip of land the length of Iowa and more, that extended from the Mississippi River inland about fifty miles. In subsequent years, they made Black Hawk similar offers and made similar purchases. The Indians moved west. One imagines Eddy joined them.

By the early 1840's, settlers started trickling into southern Iowa. The earliest ones came by flat boat to Eddy's Post (which in time morphed into Eddyville) and followed the Indian trail south into what was then called Kishkekosh Country. They encamped on the first piece of likely ground they saw, which happened to be in the northeast part of the county. These people were mostly second-generation pioneers. They were of English descent, with some Scots thrown in. All were God-fearing folks, family men, and knowledgeable farmers. Their descendants are still on the farms and are some of the finest people in the county.

Others came to Monroe County by oxen and horse, leading a milk cow behind their wagon. They crossed the Mississippi at Fort Madison and, eschewing the water route on the Des Moines River, traveled west on what is now Highway 2. These settlers came from mountain stock. They were quick, angry people, man-killers, to whom feuds were a way of life. Some of them settled in the southeastern part of the county.

The homesteaders were all given a chance to prove up on 160 acres of open ground and 160 acres of timber. If at the end of five years, the farm was sufficiently improved with adequate cabins and outbuildings, the settler was deeded the property free and clear. This was quite an opportunity for a young man, perhaps a second or third brother with little chance for an inheritance.

The trick was to get to the homestead site in early spring. The family was facing a mountain of work before cold weather. Their survival demanded shelter from the man-killing Iowa winters. The first act was to witch in a well or settle near an adequate supply of water. Then following advice from the Book of Proverbs, they cleared land, broke sod, and planted the garden before building the house.

Breaking the prairie sod and making the ground fit to plant would have been beyond the strength and will of any man, had not a blacksmith named John Deere moved to Grand Detour, Illinois. One day he curved a broken steel sawmill blade and fitted it onto a wooden plow. He hitched it onto a team and *voila!* the curved plow share allowed the soil to slide off the side of the blade. Farming just got easier. Deere quite unimaginatively labeled them "walking plows". Homesteaders nicknamed them "grasshopper plows". Some of my farmer friends have more colorful names for them.

Erecting a log cabin was a joint effort, and neighbors all pitched in. These men were experts with an axe and the best were called "corner men." A corner man's specialty was to notch the corners of the cabins, ensuring a tight fit. Cracks between logs were filled with clay and prairie grass. Fireplaces were erected from flat river rock and held together with a clay and sand mix. The roofs were flat and made from prairie sod.

Of course, the settlers suffered discomfort and heartbreak beyond our imagination. A log hut on the windswept prairie with an open draft fireplace was not much better than a windbreak, and it was a haven for mice and insects. During cold spells most folks ate, shivering by the fireplace fire, and went back to bed. That might account for the high birth rate.

The early pioneers had no health or dental care except for home remedies like putting cobwebs on open cuts and gunpowder on toothaches. Broken bones were set and the injured limb sometimes wrapped with the skin of a yellow dog. Often a disease that today could be prevented with a vaccination would take three or four children. Walk through a country cemetery sometime and read the inscriptions on the headstones.

The cabins were small cramped affairs sometimes with dirt floors. To save space, the dining table was a wide flat board hinged and hooked to the wall. It was let down to serve meals. In the summer, if the family was feeding a crowd, the front door of the cabin was taken off the hinges and used as a table.

A Dutch oven sat in every fireplace. The old black pot was used for everything from baking bread to washing clothes. A hole dug in the middle of the cabin floor was called a "bean hole." A pot of beans filled with water was placed in the hole and allowed to soften. The beans, cooked with venison or sowbelly, served as standard fare. Chairs were nonexistent. If company came, the hosts brought in field pumpkins for seating.

Most pioneers had three firearms. A heavy-caliber rifle was hung on the fireplace chimney. The heat from the fire would keep the rifle barrel dry, avoiding wet powder and a misfire. The shotgun, with powder, shot, and percussion caps handy, was kept over the front door – ostensibly to shoot anything edible. The man of the house always kept a cap-and-ball revolver loaded and by his bed. The 1840's were chancy times and people relied upon themselves.

The earliest years of homesteading were survival times. Flax was grown and beaten by a wooden device into pulp. It was woven on a spinning wheel with cotton and made almost indestructible clothes called "linsey."

The family had a team of horses, a milk cow and a garden. Farmers earmarked their swine and let them run wild. They were hardy creatures that could hold their own against sub-zero winters and wolves.

"Morning" was a term used to describe a tract of land, about the size of an acre that a team could plow in half a day. It took several years before they could break enough prairie sod to raise a serious cash crop.

Gradually life got easier. In 1845, Iowa became a state, and the county was organized and named Kishkekosh, with Albia as the county seat. Albia had its first murder that year, and the shooter was set free. Two men were arguing over two glasses of beer. One shot the other dead. When it's your turn to buy a round, you better do it, huh?

The label Kishkekosh County was a mouthful and devilishly difficult to spell. The young people made a joke of the name, calling it "kiss-me-by-gosh!" which infuriated the church elders. Through a rare stroke of bureaucratic brilliance, Kishkekosh County was soon changed to Monroe County.

The early settlers' children, the ones that survived and grew into adulthood, were hardy souls with iron constitutions. By this time, they had figured out a few things about sanitation and medical treatment. The farm was producing a cash crop. An extra room was added to the cabin. A pitched wooden shake roof replaced the sod one. Gone were the fireplaces. Families had heating stoves in the middle of the room. Sawn lumber was installed over the unsightly logs and painted white. A Singer treadle sewing machine hummed in every cabin.

As families grew older, the farmer's daughters began to receive callers. A young man knew if the girl's family liked him from the way they treated his horse. A welcome suitor would find his horse rubbed down, grained, and in a barn stall. An unwelcome suitor's horse would be left tied to the hitch rail all evening. The young man would get the point, and go courting somewhere else.

When a daughter was of marriageable age, the Singer would hum all day. The young lady's mother would make an assortment of gingham and calico dresses to wear to social occasions. Hoops for the dresses could be purchased, but were usually made from wild grape vines. If the daughter was unfortunate enough to have a face pitted from the dread smallpox, not to worry – an application of beeswax hid the scars.

When the young ladies were walking to a meeting or social occasion, they went barefoot on the road, shoes and socks in hand. A short distance from the meeting hall they would snatch a handful of prairie grass and wipe off their dusty feet, put their socks and shoes on and go inside, with shoes shined and polished.

Dances were held at a hall next to the church, or in some cases in the local schoolhouse. Box lunches were prepared in secret by the young ladies and sold. The folks would all gather around and the young men would bid for a particular box, hoping his box would belong to his favorite girl friend. No one was supposed to know which girl prepared which box. But Cupid would rear her lovely head. The auction was often rigged, and the happy couple would sit together and share lunch.

The Civil War came, and scourged Iowa. The young farm boys made good soldiers.

The hardship of growing up on an Iowa homestead made army life a lark. Iowa troops did well, fought hard, and died in astoundingly high numbers. They sailed down the Mississippi on steamboats and defeated the Confederates at Shiloh and Vicksburg, effectively cutting the Confederacy in half. The surviving Iowans followed General Sherman across the South to Atlanta, Georgia, and north through the Carolinas. In April of 1865, the South surrendered. Finally, the soldiers were mustered out of the army after the grand review parade in Washington. The boys made it back to Iowa three years after they had left.

Here you have the typical Monroe County adult male, entering the last third of the nineteenth century. Self-reliance has been instilled in him since boyhood. He has a high sense of morals and is tough as an old boot. The man has been through a major war, several financial panics, and every natural disaster except possibly an earthquake. He is uniquely prepared for the challenges ahead.

THE SCHOOLMARM

My grandmother Humeston told me about this brave school teacher, and several other ladies of her generation told the same story.   Unfortunately, over the years, names and the school site have been forgotten or lost. As well as I can determine, this incident happened several miles north of the Monroe –Appanoose County Line and west of Highway 5. I am sure this is true. Gram never lied and always got things right. Naturally, I don't know the conversations that took place, but the main facts I have presented are as they were told to me.

Prudence Mallory steps down from the sleigh and stretches, her back humped against the cold. She grasps the cheek-piece that runs between Snip's ear and mouth. With a still-warm sack lunch clamped under the left arm of her buffalo-hide coat, she turns the horses around in the trail back into the direction they had come from. A sharp "Hi-up!" sends Snip and Fanny back towards the Wallace homestead.

She never ceases to marvel that these dumb, brutish animals could find their way home without any human direction. The team knows the way to the school, too; she has proven that to herself a dozen times since she started boarding with the Wallaces.

The music of the sleigh bells over the sibilant whisper of the greased wooded runners plays a counterpoint she thinks she will never grow tired of hearing. She watches the team top the first rise and go out of sight between the snow-covered Iowa hills. After a pause to savor the moment, Prudence walks down the beaten path to the one-room log schoolhouse.

The cabin is half-warm and she can barely see her breath. The warm morning stove is radiating heat. Orion Wheatfield, one of the first to arrive, would have lit the fire and laid in a day's supply of wood. Her thirteen students sit on rough-hewn benches. They range in age from seven to fourteen, and they have hung their coats on pegs between the two windows on the north wall. Prudence walks past them to the front of the classroom. She takes off her coat and hangs it on a square nail driven into the log wall. At nineteen, her hourglass figure is encased in a gray full-length dress adorned with a double row of black shiny buttons down the front. One of the older male students looks at her breasts constantly. She is aware of his eyes and drapes a black knitted shawl over her shoulders. That done, she faces the class and says, "Good morning, students!"

They reply in unison, "Good morning, Miss Mallory!"

After leading them in the Lord's Prayer, Prudence takes several worn copies of the *Farmer's Almanac* for the older students to read and starts the others on arithmetic. One of the students, Susie Parker, sucks her thumb and plays with her doll. Her older brother, Adam, draws pictures on his slate.

Suddenly Prudence feels Will Garmon's eyes. She turns her head to face him. His leer is invasive, his eyes hot and speculating. When he tries to hold her eyes, she blushes and looks away. Prudence fears him. Will is a red-boned country boy, big for his age, with callused hands that hang like meat hooks.

Routine and the lesson plan dominate the rest of the morning. Without being told, Orion brings in more wood from the pile outside the door. When her back is turned, someone hits Adam Parker with a piece of wood. Prudence suspects Will Garmon. Partway into the morning several boys raise their hand and ask to go to the privy. She gives her permission on the condition they go one at a time. The splattered yellow snow outside the doorway is evidence boys seldom walk the thirty feet to the outhouse.

At two o'clock, Prudence can put it off no longer. She gets her coat and trudges the thirty feet through the snow to the privy. In quick, deft movements, she raises her dress and lowers her undergarments. The pitiless cold wood of the stool bites into her bare flesh like iron. In an instant she is through, undergarments up, dress down and coat on. This has to be a new speed record, she tells herself and pushes open the privy door.

It is snowing again, white cottony fluffs that portend heavy weather. To the north, lighting pulses in the heavy black clouds that blanket the sky. The rising wind whispers through the gnarled branches of the lone white oak that shades the schoolyard. Prudence shivers in her heavy coat and considers sending everybody home. She stops at the schoolhouse door and listens. Everything is quiet, so she walks around the cabin. The half-dozen ponies the boys keep to ride home stand tied in their halters, lead ropes tied to the hitching rack. The animals are skittish. Prudence knows they sense a storm.

Inside, the children are sleeping – except for Will Garmon, who is tickling a sleeping girl's face with a straw. She makes faces and wrinkles her nose.

"Will, stop that right now! Do you hear me?" Prudence demands.

"Yeah, I hear you, but I don't think I'll stop," Will answers and traces a line with the straw's end on the girl's cheekbone and nostril. "My Pa's president of the school board. Do you hear me?"

Prudence slaps his hand away and shouts, "Leave her alone!"

Will stands up and towers over Prudence. A cone of fear spreads upward from her stomach and she thinks for the first time about the brass knuckles in the bottom drawer of her desk. The students are awake and gape slack-eyed at the confrontation. Will's flushed face is twisted in anger.

"I said my Pa's president of the school board! Do you hear me?" He snarls and pushes at Prudence's chest.

She backpedals and falls, sliding on her buttocks on the puncheoned floor. There is an audible snap as her teeth click together. Prudence sits there, stunned. No one has ever hit her before. The students look on, horrified. Will stares down at her, stunned about what has happened.

He swallows and says, "My Pa is the president of the school board. Can you hear me now?"

Prudence gets to her feet, her eyes never leaving Will's. She walks back to her desk, trying to save a shred of dignity. *I'll resign tomorrow,* she tells herself, and thinks of the money she has squirreled away in her spare room at the Wallaces. *I'll travel by coach and be home in Indiana in a week. I've failed here in Iowa but no one will ever know.* She faces her students with tear-streaked eyes and they gaze back with shocked wonder.

"School's out for the day! Everybody go home!" Will Garmon announces. He steps to the wall and reaches for his coat.

Head bowed, Prudence stands behind her desk in defeat. An instinct stirs her and for the first time she hears the wind. It has increased in intensity and shrieks around the notched logs. She glances out the window and can barely see the oak tree that the schoolhouse was named for. *Do something,* she tells herself. *Do it quick or these children will leave here and surely die.*

Her right hand reaches inside the desk drawer and fumbles blindly until she finds the brass knuckles. She slips her finger into the loops. They feel like cold rings on her bare fingers and she hides her hand in the folds of her skirt. She brushes past the dressing children and blocks the door.

"No one leaves until the storm eases up. You'll all die out there!" Prudence shouts.

"Who says we won't leave? Not you!" Will snarls and pushes on her shoulders, pinning her to the door.

"You go to—" Prudence searches for the word. "You go to drat!" she finally blurts out and hits Will with a brass-knuckled jab. He staggers backward, his arms windmilling. Punching from instinct, she connects with a left hook and another brass-knuckled right cross that splinters teeth and tears his lips. Will staggers against the bench and catches himself. His right eye is swelling. Blood and bits of enamel drool from his mouth onto his shirt.

"Everybody back to their seats," Prudence says in the calmest voice she can muster. She can hear her heart beat while the children hang up coats and return to their benches. "We have a bad storm outside, students. We must stay in here until it stops. We are going to stay together all night. Won't that be fun?"

A girl comes to Prudence her face screwed and holding her crotch. "I gotta go, Miss Mallory, real bad!"

Prudence thinks for a second and makes a screen from her coat in the corner so the girls will have some privacy when they use the wood bucket. She tells the boys to tie a piece of rope around their waist and go outside to do their toilet.

Prudence's watch says four o'clock when she covertly looks at it. Through the window, the outside is a gray slate of driven snow. The wind picks up in intensity to rival an insane banshee's scream. Its icy fingers pry and tear at the notched logs. She feels a movement of air and hopes the caulking holds. She thinks, *If the roof blows off we're dead*. A mental picture forms of the children and her, crowded and frozen around a cold stove in a roofless cabin. She stamps her foot and forces the thought from her mind.

The children are pensive, huddled together in small groups. They talk quietly and are aware of the danger outside. Susie Parker sits asleep with her thumb locked in her mouth. Her brother has a protective arm around her shoulders. In the second row, Will Garmon glowers at her. He must have wiped his chin clean with fresh snow and the dried blood forms a red scarf around his neck. Behind him, Orion Wheatfield grins at her and give a thumbs-up. A warm emotion surges through Prudence and she thanks God for the Orion Wheatfields of the world.

At full dark, the children stir. They're hungry and more than a little scared. Prudence leads them in song and has them parade around the benches. Her repertoire of songs

depleted, she tells them stories. When she senses they are tired, Orion banks the fire with a hickory chunk and the children get their coats to use for blankets. After they are asleep, she lies down next to the fire and shuts her eyes. She thinks about the suitors bidding for her fried chicken at the box lunch church socials and the young attorney fresh back from the Mexican War. It would be grand to live in a fine house in Clark's Point and go to Hilton Church on Sunday in a fine red-fringed surrey and have a roast cooking at home in a Dutch oven. And forevermore! A warm bed! The bed reminds her of the attorney and carnal thoughts rush her mind. She feels her face flush and holding the brass knuckles, falls to sleep.

Prudence wakes stiff and sore from sleeping on the floor. The firs thing she hears is the wind. When it randomly probes for entry under the eaves, it reminds her of bagpipes. With her thumbnail, she scrapes a silica of ice from the window and peers out a nebulous veil of driving snow. *We're safe as long as we stay here,* she tells herself. *The storm will surely blow itself out today.*

Some snow has drifted in by her desk. She takes a handful of it and sucks it, savoring its moistness. The stove needs some attention. She throws in a couple of chunks and watches the outside bark flame.

In ones and twos, the children wake up. The girls use the bucket inside and the boys go outside tied to a rope. After some thought, Prudence starts this day as any other. Math is taught on the board and the older children read from worn books and newspapers. Will Garmon looks cowed and his swollen lips move while he makes out unfamiliar words.

At noon, Prudence peeks at the elegant pocket watch her grandfather gave her when she left Indiana. The children are hungry, crying. The wood bucket is overflowing with urine and feces and the stench is overpowering.

Her shoulders are slumping in despair when movement in the back of the room gets her attention. Orion Wheatfield has his coat half on and he frantically waves at Prudence.

She hurries to the back of the room and hears sleigh bells. Orion wrenches the door open. Prudence snatches a boy's coat from the wall and follows Orion outside.

She sees the blurred shape of Wallace's team and sleigh. On the floorboards of the sleigh sits a large Dutch oven, its top covered with an old quilt. Prudence's shout of surprise is snatched away by the wind. Together they grab the bail of the pot, lift it up and set it in the snow.

"We have to turn the team around!" Prudence shouts.

The boy nods, and Prudence sees his mouth move.

She skirts around to the front of the horses and holds onto Snip's halter. Elated, she rests her forehead on his sweaty neck and luxuriates in the warmth. Orion is beside her now, and together they pull Snip towards themselves and turn the team into the wind.

"Snip, you take care of Fanny and tell the Wallaces we're all safe, you hear?" She shouts and slaps him on the rump.

They wade knee deep in a drift and stumble over the packed snow in the trail. By chance, Prudence spies the pot, a black blob streaked white. A sudden wind gust carrying heavy snow makes her think someone had dumped a load of chicken feathers. The two pick up the oven and bonded by the iron bale, flounder towards the schoolhouse. They stumble forward blindly, imprisoned in an ethereal world of white. Within minutes, Prudence realizes they have lost their way. She smells wood smoke, which means she reasons, they are downwind from the schoolhouse. Her left arm aches with the weight of the pot. She walks on wet cold feet that feel like sponges. To sit down and rest a minute would be a blessing. Beside her Orion is a white-shrouded figure, walking slowly with his head down, the wind pushing at his back. Fondly, she thinks of the children waiting for her.

"No!" She shouts. "I won't have it!" Prudence bares her teeth at the wind and shouts, "You can't kill me! You—you goldurned son-of-a-buck! Not Prudence Mallory—I won't have it!"

Orion must have heard part of her outburst. He stops and looks at her quizzically.

"Orion—we missed the schoolhouse! We must go back and keep the wind on our left side."

He shakes his head and gestures in the direction they are going.

Prudence cups her hands around her mouth and next to his ear. "Don't you see, the wind is from the north? We are west and south of the schoolhouse. We have to go north and east. That means we must walk almost into the wind for fifty steps and then walk fifty more steps with the wind on our left side."

Orion nods his head in agreement and the two change directions.

For an eternity, they face the cruel wind that robs their breath and causes their lashes to freeze. Orion marches beside her, as steady as a well-trained draft horse. Prudence counts the steps out loud and refuses to think about her feet. Her whole universe is pain; her right arm is a spear of agony from carrying the Dutch oven. Giant shivers wrack her body. She continues beyond stubbornness, trudging into the wind.

"Forty-seven, forty-eight, forty-nine, fifty!" they count in unison, and Prudence with her free arm motions to Orion to turn right oblique.

The agony is relentless. Prudence continues one foot after the other. She stumbles, almost falls, and is braced by Orion. Resolutely they continue, the wind now on Prudence's left. She holds a mittened hand to her face and rubs her ear, cheek, and nose. The count is lost. It's warm now and she is in Indiana with her family and friends. Not in Iowa where people take off the cabin door, use it for a table, and proudly serve 'coon and snapper for dinner.

In some part of her brain, she is aware they have stopped. Prudence gropes with her hand and feels a snow-covered rough texture. This is important, she knows, but cannot remember why. Something....

"Miss Mallory," Orion shouts, "we're safe, I think! Wake up!"

Prudence shakes her head and forces herself to concentrate.

"Come on with me and leave the food here," Orion orders her and takes her wrist. He drags her around a log-notched corner and they half-fall into an open doorway. The wind is gone. Prudence takes deep inhalations of still air and exhales nosily. She crossed her forearms and beats the front of her upper arms and shoulders. Pain shoots up her legs as her circulation is restored. She looks at Orion and his blue eyes twinkle below frosted eyebrows.

"Do you know where we are?" he asks.

"N-no."

"We're in the outhouse."

Prudence smiles and laughs, a full-throated melodious sound that leaves her weak and gasping. When she recovers, she looks at Orion and they embrace. With an embarrassed expression Orion steps away and says, " I'll go around in back and get the food."

While he is gone, Prudence's mind is busy. *The privy is due east from the school and about fifty yards away,* she thinks. *I can look out the front door of the school and see the privy's front door. Therefore, if we walk towards the school with the wind up our right, we should run into the building.*

She squints at the impenetrable white curtain of snow and thinks of the misery ahead of her. *I will not be beaten,* she vows.

When Orion fills the doorway carrying the pot with both hands, she grabs the bail with her left and pushes him out the door.

"C'mon, Orion, we're not going to be found dead in a stinky privy!" she shouts.

The journey to the schoolhouse is short, and Prudence realizes if they miss the way, they will probably die in the snow. She plods forward, willing herself not to drift with the wind. Her hard-earned geometry tells her the shortest distance between two points is a straight line. She repeats the axiom while they shuffle in hip-deep snow bound together by the black pot and an iron determination. She wishes fervently she could abandon the pot.

Prudence's lashes are frozen shut again, and she lives in a whirling world of pain. Fingers of doubt probe her psyche and prod her towards a life-robbing panic. Her mind snatches at portions of prayer: "Our Father who art—who art what? Thy will be done—God, it's cold." Then through a rift in the curtain of snow, she glimpses the rectangular shape of the schoolhouse, a stone's throw away to the right.

Prudence sits on a chunk of firewood with her wet, shriveled, bare feet inches from the stove. She chews on a venison sandwich and sips a tin cup of Mrs. Wallace's vegetable stew. Susie Parker holds up a red finger, scorched from a heated stone placed inside the Dutch oven, and Prudence now knows why the pot was so heavy.

Prudence watches as one of the boys pry some chinking out from between the logs. A breath of cold fresh air wafts past her nose. The inexhaustible Orion Wheatfield, his nose wrinkled, carries the malodorous bucket of waste and empties it. Her head nods and she scarcely notices when Will Garmon covers her shoulders with his coat.

She wakes during the night and puts more wood into the stove. The children, their bellies full, sleep soundly, trusting Divine Providence and Miss Mallory. When Prudence wakes again, the room is bright. The wind is gone. Outside the window, sunlight dances on the fresh snow. She runs to the door and opens it. All across the frozen countryside, from every direction, she can hear the sound of approaching sleigh bells.

THE SORROWS OF ROSE JUDGE

The name Judge probably originated as Brehaney with perhaps a dozen different spellings. They were first found in County Kilkenny, Ireland, where they were anciently seated as judges and scholars. Judge was likely a local translation of Brehaney, a name that designated a position the family held in the Brehaney clan.

The story of Rose Judge fascinates me. She was an extremely strong woman who faced and endured hardships we can only imagine. She suffered shattering heartbreaks, losing a husband and three children in Ireland, two sons-in-law and two sons in America. Through all the anguish, she kept her family together and kept the Faith, which is still evident in her descendants today.

The scenes and background are historically accurate and I have tried to follow the Judge Chronicles in portraying Rose's life in America. No one knows the exact words they used but we can come close. The Irish idioms and prayer ejaculations in the narrative are ones I heard from my Melrose mother and Irish great-aunts.

The part about Rose receiving money from an English Lord could have been true. Many an Irish family expelled from their land were surreptitiously given money by a conscience-stricken landlord. Of course, Rose Judge had money. Travel was expensive in those days, too. Rose took four adults with her on an ocean voyage and then traveled to Harrisburg, Pennsylvania!

I put her story down in narrative form, condensing what could have been a whale of a historical novel. I got it about right, I hope. The shooting of Michael is accurate. I heard three different versions, which isn't surprising considering he was shot in 1865, and went with the most prevailing story. A special thanks to Jerry Judge, Bernard Judge, Dr. W. W. Heffron, Dr. J.J. Sheehan, Joe McGrath, Maryanne Bradley, Evelyn Tierney, and Ed Walsh, who straightened me out about Michael's murder.

Rose Judge wept when she looked back at her beloved Ireland from the deck of the leaky sailing vessel. She was leaving behind a buried husband and three sons, all killed by drunken British soldiers. There was no Mass, no burial on hallowed ground. John and their three sons were put to rest in a shallow grave next to their thatched-roof cottage. Her mind replayed the events that led up to her leaving Ireland.

A fortnight ago, she and her family of four had been evicted. A British noblewoman who needed more land to foxhunt had seventy families expelled from their little farms and sent on the road.

That afternoon, an English gentleman riding a fine horse pulled Rose out of a procession of several hundred homeless people. The lord acted angrily, jammed his mount between her and the crowd. He placed an index finger to his lips and draped a purse with a long leather strap over her head. Rose recognized the clicking as the sound of gold coins. She adjusted the strap around her neck and pushed the purse under her bodice. The Englishman winked at her and made the sign of the cross. In wonderment, she blessed herself, and after he rode away, scurried back to her family.

That night the procession stopped in a chilling rain. Behind the protective backs of sons John and James, Rose sprinkled the coins onto her apron and tried to count them. She was unsure of some of the larger denominations and guessed at the total. But this much was certain: a double handful of English sovereigns was enough for a fresh start in America. All she had to do was suffer the hardships and get her family to a port city.

It was been difficult, but they endured it – buoyed by the travel fare to America that bounced between Rose's breasts.

And now, standing on the tilting deck of the *Celestia* with their passage paid, Rose wiped tears from her eyes with a new handkerchief and smiled when son John put his arm around her. Behind her, James Judge guarded the luggage. An arm's length away Bridget and Michael exchanged words and laughed. Bridget already looked seasick.

The boat lurched at an errant wave and cold seawater lashed Rose's face. She turned to her friend Kate Hussey, who stood staring at the receding shoreline and fingering her beads.

"Did you see Sean in the crowd?" she asked.

"No," Rose said. "I'm sorry."

"He told me to go on if he didn't show up. Sean told me he would catch a boat and come later. The Brits have him, I can feel it," Kate said and dropped her rosary in her coat pocket. "Sean fought them, blood for blood, he used to say."

Rose thought of captured priests dipped in tar and hung from lampposts or trees until their rotted bodies fell to the ground.

"Sean is a smart lad, and a brave one, too. He'll make it. Probably will be over on the next boat. Say a payer for him," she said and squeezed Kate's hand.

"All right, you Irish scum, get down below deck!" A pig-tailed sailor wearing First Mate's pips shouted and pointed to an open hatch. "You'll get food twice a day and a fresh bucket for bodily wastes twice a day. Any of you Papists don't like it down there, let us know. We'll throw the blighter overboard."

Rose took John's arm and started down the stairs. The interior was gloomy and the air fetid. Bilge water splashed under the planked floor. A rat scurried across the floor in front of them.

"Here we go, children. This will be our home for the next six weeks," Rose said and tried to smile.

AMERICA

The City of New York looked dismal in the late morning sun. Some of the taller buildings were shrouded in coal smoke. An offshore breeze carried the stench of sewage and a nearby tannery. *It smells better than our home in the cellar of this Godforsaken boat, I'll give it that,* Rose thought.

Bodies pressed on her from all sides as fifty Irishmen gulped the air and vied for a glimpse of their new country. A careless boot heel stamped her toes and she reminded herself to be patient.

"Rose," Kate Hussey said and pulled her sleeve.

"Kate, praise be to God, we're here at last," Rose said.

"What will I do? The captain refused to return Sean's half of the fare. Said it wasn't his fault. Rose, I don't have any money," Kate said.

"Now you do," Rose said and gave her a dozen coins.

"Rose, I–" Kate started to speak and her eyes teared.

"Go on with you." Rose grinned and joined the line leaving the boat.

"Judge!" the First Mate shouted, and Rose's family started down the gangplank.

"Irish pigs! Bloody Papists!" British sailors shouted. A smaller group spit on them and yelled obscenities at Bridget. The three Judge men faces were bladed with anger. Bridget's cheeks flamed scarlet in embarrassment. Rose marched past the taunting sailors, her head held high. "Irish are the best!" she shouted and stepped onto the dock.

"Where we going now, Mum?" John asked as they walked towards the street.

"I'm not sure, John," Rose answered.

A heavy wagon containing wheelbarrows and shovels clattered past them. A crudely painted sign attached to the wagon's sideboard said HELP WANTED—IRISH NEED NOT APPLY.

"But I don't think this is the town for us," she concluded and stepped onto the board sidewalk.

The muddy street ahead of them seemed impossible to cross. Lumbering dray wagons vied for advantage with each other. A stagecoach pulled by six black horses flashed past. A rider, leading two paint ponies, stopped and tipped his hat at Bridget. To Rose's right a mule, part of a team pulling a wagon load of barrels, squatted in the road and refused to go further. The street became a writhing sea of stalled, cursing drivers and trumpeting mules.

"This way," Rose pointed to a gap between the wagons. She skirted a pool of raw sewage and led her family across the street.

"Now what, Mum?" James asked and wiped manure from his boots with a hank of wind-blown straw.

"Now we find a decent hotel with beds and good food and have real baths," Rose told them.

"Hey, there's one right down the street," Michael said and jabbed an index finger towards a stone building

"Don't point, Mike. That's bad manners. You want people to think you just got off the boat?" Rose demanded and led her family towards the Ritz Hotel.

The desk clerk, with a show of reluctance, peered at Rose over wire-rimmed glasses.

"I want two rooms and warm baths drawn. Send a laundress for our clothes. I also want a pot of hot tea," Rose told him and placed a gold coin on the counter.

"Right away, ma'am." The animated clerk signaled a bellhop and handed Rose the registry book and pen.

Rose signed her name in a flourish and followed her family upstairs. Late that night, she woke in a warm feather bed, having dreamt she was in the hold of that terrible ship. Bridget slept beside her, the three men in the next room. Rose was warm and clean and full of good food.

This New York is no place for my family, she thought. *And I better get my boys to work before they grow lazy.*

In Ireland Sheila Murphy had told her Harrisburg, Pennsylvania was a fine place with lots of Irish, a new church, and work to be had. *Maybe we'll just go there, wherever Pennsylvania is. These Americans have strange names for places. By rightful reason they should have named it something civilized like Armagh. Oh well, God will provide.*

HARRISBURG

The journey to Harrisburg was uneventful. The coach stopped every twenty miles to change horses. The food was excellent; home-cooked meals with steaming carrots and potatoes. Rose liked the meat and was surprised to find out it was deer. The family stayed one night in an inn and arrived in Harrisburg late the next morning.

An Irish priest told them of a run-down cabin on the river's edge that could be bought for a song. Rose took her family to it and saw a small log hut with a stone fireplace. A planked board hung against a bare wall, held there by hinges and a hook. The owner told her that at mealtime the snap was released and the board swung down to for a dining table. Rose made the deal and ordered Bridget and Michael to start cleaning. She sent John and James out to find jobs.

The Judges drew water from the river that also contained sewage and garbage from the cabins upstream. Their iron constitutions saved them. The family suffered little more than colds. A neighbor told her the river was called the Susquehanna. Again, Rose shook her head in wonder at the strange American names.

Rose sat on the porch of her new home and thought it was time for the family to have some fun. She studied the area in front of her cabin. Through a quirk in geology, the ground lay smooth, blanketed with flat river rock and sand. It would be a grand place to dance. Some windfall trees behind the cabin could be trimmed and dragged around in front. They would make good enough seats. It should work. John could sort of play the fiddle, she recalled. She sent Bridget to town to buy a fiddle.

On her way home Bridget met some ladies from the parish. When asked about the new fiddle, she said it was for her brother John and that Mum had found a grand place to dance—right in front of their cabin.

That afternoon Rose looked out her cabin door and saw two men roasting a deer carcass over a wood fire at the edge of Rose's dance floor. "It looks as if we're going to have a dance," she told her new cat. An hour later three ladies arrived with two Dutch oven full of potatoes. At their instructions, the men shoveled hot wood coals on the black pots. Rose invited the ladies in and made tea. They were all first cousins and from County Clare. Clare people she could abide, they were much nicer than the stiff-necked omathans from Cork.

By darkness, a hundred celebrants were there. Campfires ringed the dance floor. A full moon rose over the Susquehanna River and a trio of fiddlers played Irish tunes. The people danced until the moon set and a pink cast brightened the eastern sky. Liam Purcell, a one-armed veteran of the American-Mexican War, sang in a fine tenor voice of a home that never was. The dancers joined in the chorus, cried, and had a grand time.

James prospered at his job driving a dray wagon and met a young woman named Maryanne Sheehan at a church box lunch social. The pair started seeing each other, and Rose decided to build another addition onto their house. That fall the two were married at Saint Patrick's church and moved into the new room. That night another dance was held at the Judge cabin.

The lovely Bridget fell in love with a man named Patrick Mulligan. One Sunday afternoon, after late Mass, Patrick came to Rose and asked her for permission to marry her daughter. He had to shout to be heard, because John was practicing his fiddle and Mike blew sounds from a harmonica that sounded like a wounded banshee.

Rose smiled and rocked. She already knew of Patrick's background, that he came from a good family in Ireland, and she felt her husband John would approve. He was from County Cork, but she decided not to hold that against him. Rose agreed to the wedding and offered to build them a room onto the cabin. Patrick smiled, seemed to think about it, and graciously declined.

The next two years went well for the Judges. John got a promotion on his job. He wore a fine black suit to Mass on Sunday, ushered, and rang the bell. James and Maryanne had a daughter named Roseanne. Patrick and Bridget produced a girl named Eliza. Michael took his first step towards citizenship.

That winter tragedy struck. Patrick was helping a group of men cut ice on the Susquehanna. He slipped and fell through a hole into the swirling waters. His body was never recovered. Bridget and Eliza moved back in with Rose.

Bridget hated the river and couldn't stand to look at it. She had nightmares of Patrick trapped under the ice. Then there were Rose's sons; they were restless and wanted land of their own. A cousin of Patsy Murphy's lived in Melrose, Iowa, and he knew all about homesteading, John said. Iowa was a new state and had farmland free for proving up on it.

Late one night Rose sat by the fireplace. Her mind was restless. Her sons want to farm and have land of their own. Bridget hated Pennsylvania after losing her husband.

Rose got her purse from its hiding place in the fireplace and counted the coins. This house would sell for a tidy profit, she reckoned. Maybe it was time to move. She'd sleep on it.

The next morning at the breakfast table she announced, "Let's plan on getting out of here before spring."

"Where are we going?" Bridget asked.

"Iowa," Rose said.

"Where's Iowa?" Bridget asked.

"That way," Rose said and pointed west.

The three brothers whooped and pounded each other on the back. The babies woke and started to cry.

IOWA

Clinton, Iowa was a lot like Harrisburg, Rose decided. Both towns had large Irish-Catholic populations and prices at the market seemed reasonable. And thanks be to God, John found a three-bedroom home with sod already broke for a large garden! It was far enough away from the river that Bridget didn't have to look at it and be reminded of her poor dead husband. This river was a big one, Rose said when she saw it and repeated "Mississippi" over again until her tongue got around it. Again, she wished her husband John was with them. They would have fun with that impossible name.

Her sons didn't stay with her long. Financed in part by coins from her purse, they traveled into south central Iowa and homesteaded near Bedford in Taylor County. She wept when they left, but she still had Bridget and Eliza. One Sunday at Mass, she was amazed to meet Kate Hussey, whom she hadn't seen since New York City. Kate immediately paid off her debt and loaned her a brindle milk cow.

A year went by, and Bridget married a likely looking man named Francis Moran. Rose's sons came back for the wedding, but once they were gone again, she missed them. Letters from them were intermittent. Through Herculean efforts, the three Judge men had built cabins and broken sod. The Iowa land was rich and yielded bountiful crops. Still Rose worried about John and Michael. It was time they were married. She would have to look around. Maggie Cooney's oldest daughter, Catherine, was of marrying age. Hmm. It might do to have Maggie over for tea after Mass.

In September of 1856, John and Catherine were married in Clinton. At the wedding, son Michael danced at least a dozen times with Francis Moran's sister, Ellen. In the week Michael was home, he spent more time with Ellen than with his own mother. Rose smiled and thought she wouldn't have to play matchmaker this time. Michael returned to Clinton every month. John said he wore out two good horses courting Ellen. The couple married in May of 1858 and left by stage the next morning. Michael had to get to his homestead. There was corn to plant.

It was July 26, 1860 and an uncommonly hot summer, Rose would remember later. She was sitting on her porch snapping beans. Kate Hussey and her husband Sean, accompanied by Father Mackey, walked up her lane. Kate hurried to Rose and put her arm around. Sean and Father Mackey stopped on the steps and removed their hats.

"Bad news, is it? " Rose asked. "Out with it!"

"Missus Judge, it's your son-in-law. He dropped dead on the street. The doctor claim it was a brain tumor brought on by the vapors," the priest said.

"Dear God!" said Rose and threw her apron over her head. The beans forgotten, she rocked in the chair and cried softly.

"Where's Bridget?" she asked, her voice muffled by the apron.

"Mag Noonan is bringing her and Eliza over here by the by," Kate said.

"There's work to be done," Rose said and lowered her apron. " Sean, will you do me a favor?"

"Name it."

"Go to Francis and Bridget's place. Get Francis' best suit and take it to the undertaker. I want him laid out in a nice box. We'll have the wake tonight and funeral in the morning, if that's fine with you, Father," Rose said.

"Fine, Missus Judge. That's the way we'll do it. C'mon, Sean, we better get going," Father Mackey said.

"Stay here with me a while, Kate," Rose said and rocked furiously. "Oh, my poor, poor, Bridget."

That night after Bridget and Eliza had gone to sleep, Rose stepped out on the porch. An inner urge plagued her. The air carried the fish scent of the river and fireflies blinked under the trees. Lord, she needed to rest.

A husband and three children lay buried in Ireland. A son-in-law drowned and never to have a Christian burial. And now, Francis, the one whom she doted upon, dead from the vapors.

She sat in her chair and rocked. There was a war coming soon, she could feel it. The politicians were talking, stirring up the people, and young men were marching. It was time to move to Bedford. She could stay with John, and Bridget got along better with Michael. She would write John a letter tomorrow.

BEDFORD

Taylor County was a sight different from the river country, Rose told Eliza. The land here was hilly, covered with trees and blessed with springs. The three farms were just as grand as the brothers said they were. They sprawled next to each other and were bound with split-rail fences. Most of their ground lay flat and in places held a shovel-handle length of rich black soil. None of their neighbors were Irish-Catholic, but the closest ones, two Scottish cousins named Macintosh, seemed friendly enough and often shared work with them. A priest came around once a month, stayed with James, and said Mass.

The war soon started, just as Rose thought, and the butchery commenced, some on the Iowa-Missouri border. Soldiers in blue uniforms stopped at their house and Maryanne gave them water while their horses rested in the shade of an oak tree. Sometimes the blue-clad cavalry came north from Missouri, and men rode past who were bandaged or wrapped in rubber sheets and bent over a saddle. Other times riders wearing parts of military uniforms came from the south. They were heavily armed and rode like they were part horse. They were rough men, profane and impolite, who took apples without asking. Her sons all bought muskets, Rose noticed, and kept their livestock close to the house.

At planting time in 1865, Angus Macintosh stopped on the road. From horseback he cupped his hands and shouted, "the war is over! Lee surrendered at Appo – appo something-or-other down south."

Rose and Maryanne looked up from their garden work and smiled.

Rose blessed herself and said, "Thanks be to God the killing is over." 63

Macintosh walked his horse over to the edge of the garden and dismounted. He removed his hat and said, "Don't dance about too quick, Missus Judge. There are people around here who aim to have your farms. Expect trouble when their lads get home."

"This land is ours! Why would anyone want what we have worked for?" Maryanne asked.

"That's the way the world is, Ma'am," Macintosh said. "Ain't that right?"

"I'm afraid so," Rose said and decapitated a weed with her hoe. "I'm afraid so."

The trouble didn't start until the corn was knee-high. Saturday afternoon was sale day and the hamlet of Bedford bustled. While the men bought or sold livestock, the women did their shopping. When Rose and her daughters-in-law went into the general store they were met with cold stares and silence from people they had known for years. Mister Goematt, the storeowner whispered to Rose from across the counter. "We can't do business after today, Missus Judge. No Catholics allowed. I'm very sorry."

Shocked, Rose doubled the amount on her shopping list. She handed it to Hilda Goematt and felt a pang when Hilda refused to meet her eyes. In silence, and aloof as stone statues, the Judges waited while their order was filled. Rose closed out their account and marched out of the store, her daughters-in-law and grandchildren in tow. Her sons, all thee on horseback, were waiting at the wagon. James hunched in his saddle, glowering at passers-by. Michael sat upright, slamming a fist into his open palm.

"You know those six heifers we brought to the sale? Well, somebody hamstrung them when they were back in the pens," John said.

"Oh, no," Maryanne said and put her hands to her cheeks.

"God in heaven!" Rosa exclaimed. "What will happen next? Boys, get down from your horses and load these supplies."

"Ma, what did you do—buy out the store?" John asked.

"I had to. They won't trade with us anymore because we are Catholics. I bought up enough sundries to last us a spell and settled the account," Rose said.

"I think I'll go see Fritz Goematt and settle another account," Michael said.

"I think you won't, Michael. You point that horse towards home and go there right now. James, turn the team so we won't have to go by the stock sale," Rose ordered.

James grabbed the cheek-piece on the near horse and turned the wagon and team back in the direction from which they had come. He unsheathed his musket and holding it upright, its brass butt plate resting on his thigh, followed his family towards their homesteads.

That evening a horseman galloping past on the road and screeching the Rebel yell, shot into John's cabin. The bullet gouged their tabletop and broke one of Maryanne's favorite plates. Around midnight, a stack of rails James had cut to use for fencing caught fire. The blaze from the seasoned hickory illumined the western sky. A day later James Judge surprised two men in his back pasture. They had torn down a section of rail fence and were chousing his team towards the gap. He shouted at them and shots were exchanged. Michael and John had to come down and stand guard while James and Maryanne lifted rails back into place.

Angus Macintosh and his cousin Andrew rode to John's farm and stopped on the road. Rose noticed both men were armed with side arms and muskets. John hurried down the path to his friends. From his body language, Rose knew they were in an intense conversation. Rose got up from her rocker and went to them.

"Some ruthless men want your farms and will use the excuse that you are Catholic to run you off or kill you. You are the only three Catholic families in the county. Nobody is going to look after you. Your best deal is to go to the bank and put these farms up for sale. You've improved these places enough, Lord knows. You fellows can walk away with some serious money," Angus said.

Both Scots tipped their hat and said in unison. "Morning, Missus Judge."

Rose nodded her head and listened.

"Listen, John. Since the end of the war, bloody-minded men have been running the hills. They were bushwhackers during the war, and killing means nothing to them," Andrew said. "For a five-dollar gold piece, they'd kill you all. The word on the street says someone is fixing to hire them to run you Judges off or worse. "

"We can fight them," John said. "They can't have my land. I earned this place. It's mine!"

"Yeah, you fight them and mayhap a stray bullet hits your daughter. Is your farm worth that?" Angus demanded.

Rose heard all she needed. She nodded good-bye to the Macintosh cousins and turned away. She walked into their cabin and shut the door.

Enough is enough, Rose thought. After the Macintosh cousins left, she called her family together.

Rose sat at the head of the table and felt the familiar glow of having her entire family with her. Her three daughters-in-law sat across from her: Catherine, pregnant again and Maryann nursing a baby. Ellen, her favorite, rubbed her work-roughened hands together. Bridget made a hushing signal to Eliza and pointed her towards the other children. Behind them, her sons lounged against the log walls. All three of them were handsome, Rose thought, all tall muscular men with the blue eyes and black hair of the Irish. James looked a lot like her long-dead husband and again, she wished he were here to see them. On the fireplace hearth, her grandchildren played with a basket of kittens.

"It's time to move," Rose said. "We stay here and some of us will get killed."

An outraged silence screamed though the cabin. The family froze in positions of astonishment. Ellen drummed her fingers on the tabletop and seemed engrossed in the stone fireplace chimney behind Rose. One of the men cleared his throat.

Finally John spoke. "I don't know, Mum. We just got title on our farms. They belong to us free and clear. We can't just walk away from them."

"We won't walk away from anything. You go into the bank tomorrow and make your best deal. Tell them we want paid in gold coin, not paper money," Rose said. "There's a farm agent named Lassiter. He buys land, too. See what he will give you."

"I think of all the work we've done and…" James said.

"I left a husband and three sons dead in Ireland," Rose said. She stood up, her face mottled with anger, and shook her finger at them. "I buried a son-in-law in Harrisburg and another in Clinton. I do not aim on leaving another member of this family in a lonely grave!"

"I hate to run away from a fight," John said.

"You are not running away from a fight. Only a fool would stay here against these odds," Maryanne said.

"John, I'm your wife and I don't want to be a widow. You want me to have to raise Roseanne by myself?" Catherine said.

"No, no not at all," John said and looked at his two brothers. "What do you think?"

"Plenty of land," Michael shrugged.

"Let's make the deal tomorrow and maybe these people will leave us alone. Let the buyer take possession December first. That gives us time to get the crops out and have a sale before the winter gets bad," James said.

"In the meantime we can look around and find some place to homestead around our own people," John said.

"That priest that came through here last week said they're building a grand Catholic church at Staceyville, and there's land south of there open for homesteading," Rose said.

"I know where Staceyville is. We'll have to get over there soon as we can and look around," John said.

"Then it's settled?" Rose said.

"Yes, it's settled," John said.

The other two brothers made sounds of agreement. Rose's daughters-in-law nodded and smiled their agreements. *Saints be praised,* Rose thought, *we're going to move to Staceyville.* It would be nice to get back with the Irish. Besides, she missed the sounds of the fiddles.

THE SALE

An early morning crow jeered as John went from his log barn towards the cabin. It had snowed during the night, and a white skiff covered the frozen ruts of the trail. The air carried the scent of wood smoke mingled with frying bacon. At the door of his cabin, he stopped and looked back. This was the last time he would see this farm as his own. He felt a tinge of regret. Tomorrow ownership passed to a stranger.

He and Michael had filed on adjoining homesteads in Monroe County. They could help each other. James was going to Kansas. *Ah well, he'll come back. Better eat breakfast and get ready for the sale.* It was going to be a long day.

James and Michael had driven their livestock up to John's corral and were brushing and currying the horses when buyers started drifting in. These savvy men watched the milling animals with expert eyes and mentally set their top price before the adrenaline rush of the auctioneering. John nodded to several of them and walked to his corral.

Two men came out of his barn and the tall one said something funny. They both laughed and looked at John. A jolt of red rage fueled him. John started towards the men when someone grabbed his arm.

"It's a fine day for a sale, and don't be letting those blighters get the best of you."

John looked around and saw Angus Macintosh. The brawny Scot squeezed John's arm and walked him away from the crowd. They stopped next to the wagons.

"I see you have your wagons loaded," Macintosh said.

"Yes, we want out of here as soon as we can."

"Well, leaving your teams and saddle horses in my corral is smart. That way there can be no confusion."

"I hope not," John told him. He shielded his eyes against the eastern sun and saw a score of men in buggies and twice that many on horseback approaching on the north road.

"Listen to me, John. A lot of people around here know your family was done dirt. They will see that you-all get out of here safe," Macintosh said. "Don't let what some fool says rile you, hear?"

"Yes," John said and started to leave.

"One more thing. If those Longriders show up, be hard rock careful," Macintosh said.

"I will. Thanks for the advice," John said and started towards the crowd of buyers.

The sale started with a miscellany of furniture, hand tools, harnesses, and old walking plows. That done, the crowd followed the auctioneer into James' barn where they sold their sheep, chickens, geese, and bee hives. The bidding was spirited, most items selling for full value. By noon, the sale moved to the livestock corralled next to John's cabin. The crowd was subdued, perhaps a hundred men wrapped in fur or Union Army coats stood in small groups and spit tobacco. They wore their collective guilt like a shroud and refused to meet the Judge brothers' eyes.

The buyers ringed the corral. The auctioneer stood on a barrel crying the sale and watching for bids. Michael led the livestock, one at a time, around the periphery of the corral. The Judge women's faces were pasted to the cabin windows as they watched seven years of work being sold away.

John leaned on the rail fence, away from the buyers. His moods alternated from rage to acceptance, from elation to despair. *Family safety is more important than land,* he told himself. He looked out at the ground he had toiled on for so long and brought to fruition and wondered if he could ever summon up the will to do this again. Yes, he knew he could. He would transform raw land into a paying farm again and even again if he had to. *This piece of bad luck is not going to break me,* he resolved.

Then the sale was over. Men worked faster now, loading equipment and herding livestock in the fading Iowa twilight. Rose, swathed in a buffalo coat, and James in a sheepliner, were settling accounts with the auctioneer. Eliza had just come out on the front porch of the cabin. John looked up to see the five Longriders join the crowd. Two of them dismounted. One carried a blanket. The other held a revolver half concealed by his duster. They walked towards Michael.

"Hey, Mike!" John shouted. "Look out!"

"You one of them Catholics?" the one with the revolver asked.

"Yes, I'm Catholic," Michael said.

The nearest Longrider threw the blanket over Michael. Michael raised his hands, fighting the blanket. The other Longrider stepped closer and shot Michael in the head.
68

"The men in the long coats just shot Uncle Mike!" Eliza screamed from the porch.

"Noooo!" John shouted and lunged at the killer with a pitchfork.

At point-blank range, the Longrider aimed his revolver at John's chest and fired. The weapon misfired. Cursing, the killer evaded John's pitchfork and re-cocked his revolver. Men crowded between them, forcing the Longriders back. A Longrider on horseback spat an order and the other two swung into the saddle.

"John—get your family into your cabin before they kill you all!" Andrew Macintosh yelled.

James and Rose were somehow beside him. He hurried them to the cabin and shooed Eliza off the porch. Inside, John took his shotgun down from over the door and loaded it, put percussion caps on the cones, and set the hammers on half-cock. James primed his musket and went to the window. The women and children wailed their grief in an age-old dirge.

An hour after full dark someone rapped on the door.

"Who is it?" John said.

"It's Angus Macintosh," His voice sounded muffled through the board door. "Listen to me. The Longriders might come back and burn you out. Turn your lamps down so they can't see a light from the windows. Maybe they'll think you've lit out."

"What about Mike?" James asked.

"Mike's dead. I'll box him up and put him on sawhorses in my barn. You can come back and get him after this cools down. Be ready to go at first light," Angus said.

"All right."

STACEYVILLE

When Rose first saw her new home site, she thought it was just a clearing at the edge of the trail. But after being helped down from the wagon, she noticed a well had been dug and a puncheon floor laid. Trimmed and sized logs lay in nearby stacks. Someone had split wooden shakes for the roof and at least a cord of them were stacked between two trees. John had this done when he staked out the homestead. What foresight! His father would have been proud. John had earned the title of "himself."

The first morning, neighbors streamed in with axes and horses. Rose watched these men who were experts with an axe and inured to discomfort work on the snow-pelted ground, their breath pluming in their faces. She smiled at the chunk of axes and the shouts of men to their horses, for she knew her cabin would be up in jig time. Before the roof was finished a dray clear from Albia arrived with a new stove. They set it up in the

St. Patrick's Church, Georgetown (formerly Staceyville)

center of the cabin. It was a grand stove boasting the name WARM MORNING with shiny knobs to polish.

The housewarming was blighted, though. John borrowed a spring wagon and accompanied with a new-found friend went to Bedford after Michael. He returned on a bright winter morning. They held a wake that night at the cabin and had a funeral Mass for Michael the next day at the Georgetown Corners. Half the worshipers sat outside or in huddled in their wagons and trailed in at Communion time. At the grave, Rose, for a quicksilver of time, saw her dead husband next to the dirt pile. On the way home, John took his family around the new church to inspect the progress.

In the summer of 1869, the new church was completed and the Bishop came for the dedication ceremony. Rose never saw a bishop before, so she got to Mass early to see one up close. She was surprised. He didn't look like anything special. After Mass, there was a picnic on the lawn. As soon as the Bishop left, they broke out the fiddles.

Time flew on winged feet for Rose. She was happy, enjoying days she hoped would never end. Bridget's daughter, Eliza, married a likely-looking Irish lad, and a year later Rose witnessed her great-granddaughter baptized in the new church. John's family continued to grow, and James wrote to them regularly.

That spring, in 1874, Rose started to fail. She was seventy-eight and the oldest

St. Patrick's Cemetery, Georgetown. The Judge family stone is at far left.
The church spire is visible through the trees.

woman in the parish. She needed help getting into the buggy, and the thought of getting old hit her like a lightning bolt. The priest reminded her that longevity was a mark of a holy life.

One summer afternoon, Rose rocked in the dappled shade at the edge of the vegetable garden. She was tired and had to ask Bridget to help her to her chair. Bees from son John's hives toiled in the nearby apple orchard, and blossoms fell in a blizzard of pink petals. It reminded her of a pleasant memory beyond her remembering. What was it—if only she could recall....

She had put the leather purse that British officer had given her somewhere. It still contained a few gold English sovereigns. *Oh well, someone will find it in their time of need*. The money wasn't that important. The family was together.

Yesterday she thought she saw her long dead husband John among the apple trees, and she had told Bridget. Bridget had smiled, nodded her head and continued scrubbing clothes. *Well, today I'll just watch for him*, Rose decided.

She touched the worn rosary beads in her apron pocket. They were the same beads she had prayed crossing the ocean and half a continent.

A south breeze teased her nostrils. Rose inhaled the aroma of green plants and the promise of new life. The same breeze ruffled the apple leaves and Rose thought she saw movement. Aha! There was somebody moving between the trees, and it was John! He walked through the garden, being careful to stay between the rows, and stopped in front of her. He looked grand wearing a blue broadcloth suit with a white rose in his lapel. His face was unlined and his black hair was slicked down. He reached out with his hand and she took it. Then Rose was on her feet, feeling a light and spry as a girl.

"Where are you taking me, John?" she asked coquettishly.

"Back through the apple trees. I have something to show you. It's a surprise," John smiled and led her through the garden.

Drive partway back in Saint Patrick's Cemetery at Georgetown. Stop by an old wind-twisted cedar tree. The Judge family stone is under the tree. The original limestone markers are gone, eroded by wind and nicked by mowers. But Rose Judge rests there with her family, John and Catherine Judge, James and Mary Anne Judge, Michael and Ellen Judge.

Tony Humeston

THE LONG WAY HOME

In the spring of 1844 Roland Ingham, his wife, Genevieve, and their two sons came from Indiana to Monroe County. They settled on a one-hundred-sixty-acre patch of land which Roland had bought for the princely sum of one dollar an acre. The first winter they suffered a frontier accident, which necessitated Roland returning to Fort Madison for supplies. He started home with his team and sledge, and what happened next is an astounding true story of one man's indomitable will in a struggle with one of the worst blizzards of the century.

Roland survived the ordeal and prospered, dying almost twenty years later. I read his will at the courthouse. Roland had a good education for the times. His penmanship is cursive, his sentence structure and grammar flawless.

Nagging questions remain: He and his wife, both in their forties, have two young sons. Why did they marry so late in life? Roland had a decent education and obviously some money. Why did they leave Indiana? Why did they come to Iowa and choose a life of drudgery?

Roland leaped from the sledge and ran to the open door of their cabin when he heard Genevieve's scream. Over his wife's shoulder, he peered inside and gawked in disbelief. Fresh hatchet marks scarred their smashed furniture. Gleaming shards of white china freckled an insane mosaic pattern on the fireplace hearth. An irregular coating of flour covered their puncheoned floor and broken table. A stoved-in keg of sorghum lay upside down on their shredded feather tick mattress.

Roland reacted first. He drew his revolver and stepped into the room. Broken pottery snapped under his boots. The hickory coals in the fireplace had gone out and the room was cold. The spilled sorghum had started to congeal on the bed.

The vandals were gone. The room was safe.

Roland lowered his gun and shut his eyes, trying to comprehend the enormity of the damage.

"If I get hold of the son-of-a-bitch that did this, I'll kill him!" he grated.

"Shh," Genevieve was beside him clutching his arm. "Don't say that."

"Gen, everything we have—anything of any use or value – has been ruined or stolen."

"The cow! Roland, see to the cow, we have to have milk!"

Roland whirled and ran to the barn. Seconds later, he returned and leaned against the open door frame.

"They killed the cow.... took the loins. All our smoked meat's gone too," he said and gazed at the marks of unshod pony hoovesd that pockmarked the snow in front of the cabin.

"Who in the world would do something like this to us?" Genevieve asked. Her hazel eyes bored into his.

"The Goddamned Indians you fed and let use our well all summer. It's a wonder they didn't burn us out," Roland told her.

"Swearing is never necessary, especially when you have just come from church, Mister Ingham."

"Sorry," Roland muttered.

"We have to do something right now. Those boys will have to have food for the winter or they'll die!" Genevieve said.

Roland spoke slowly and deliberately. "First, you bring the boys in from the sledge while I build a fire."

Roland busied himself with flint and steel and soon coaxed a steady blaze. When he straightened, their two sons were playing in one corner while Genevieve swept the floor.

"I'm going to Fort Madison," he said.

"There's no other way, is there?"

"No, there's no other way," Roland said and thought of the hard one-day trip to Fort Madison. Genevieve stopped sweeping the floor and looked at him. Roland handed her his cap and ball revolver.

"You keep this.I have the rifle. I'll be back in three—four days," Roland said and smiled. "I'll bring you back some new cups, too."

"You'll need some food for the way," Genevieve said.

"I'll stop at the Roushes' and tell them what happened. They'll give me some food and be over to help you clean up quick as you can say *Jack Robinson!*"

"Oh, Roland, I know you have to go, but be careful," Genevieve said.

They embraced briefly. Roland, after a long look at his wife and family, went to his sledge.

"I'll be back for you all," he vowed and mounted the sledge. He turned the team toward the trail and took a long look at his wife and two sons, silhouetted in the cabin door. *Genevieve is worried,* he thought. *I can see it in her face. She'll try and hide it from the two boys. I better say something.*

"They claim it's eighty miles to the trading post!" Roland shouted. "Don't worry! Ebb and Flow is the best team in Kishkekosh Country. I'll be there tomorrow afternoon!"

The next afternoon, Roland reined up in front of the trading post at Fort Madison. He flipped off the buffalo robe and stiffly climbed down from the sledge box. His body ached, for he was forty-four in an era when that was considered old. After stamping his boots in the stained snow, he climbed the split-log steps and stepped into the trading post.

Roland made his purchases and remembered to buy a set of dishes for Genevieve. The trader, a happy Frenchman named Jacques LeDeau, dickered with him over the price. They settled and gold coins thunked on the barrel-head. Le Deau handed him a sack of horehound candy that had been spiced with peppermint. The two men laughed and watched while two young squaws dressed in identical blue gingham dresses loaded his sledge.

Roland drove Ebb and Flow into a large barn constructed from sawn lumber someone had surely stolen from the army. After unharnessing the geldings, a grizzled old trapper showed him two vacant stalls. He rubbed the horses down and grained them while the old man carried water. Roland flopped down on a pile of fresh straw and instructed the old man to wake him for supper.

At first light, Roland hitched his team and made ready to go. The old trapper followed him outside, working on a fresh chew and spitting tobacco juice at a barn cat.

"How far you going?" he asked.

"Kishkekosh Country. I'll be home after dark, I get a move on," Roland said.

"I was you, I'd wait a day or so. Snowstorm coming in," the old man said and worked the chew into his left cheek.

"Can't. I got a family at home that might be getting hungry," Roland told him.

"They'll be a damned sight hungrier if you don't get home at all," the old man said.

"Got to go now. See you green-up time!" Roland said and grinned.

"Uh-huh."

Roland slapped the reins and the team started westward. From long habit, he let the horses walk the first hundred yards and then urged them into a trot. They traveled on an Indian trail that skirted a ragged fringe of trees bordering an unknown stream. The morning sun warmed Roland's back and the air was crisp. A doe flushed from a nearby deadfall, her white tail flagging with alarm. She ran ahead of the team briefly before disappearing into a stand of cedars. To the north, a black line of clouds limned the horizon.

Hours later the ground fell away, and the trail wove through buck brush and spindly trees. Trail-wise, the horses slowed to a walk and stopped in a wide clearing. Roland stepped over a ring of firestones and opened the hinged door on a wooden box that hung from a giant cottonwood. There were four letters addressed to people in Clark's Point. He stuffed them in his pocket and led his team across the river's ice. The other riverbank was bare. Roland *geed* and *hawed* the horses between cabin-sized stones and past charred stumps. The team pulled up a mile-long grade with ease. They topped a rise and were out of the Des Moines River Valley. Roland faced a sea of white; an endless gentle roll of hills that stretched westward. Ebb and Flow trotted with a renewed vigor. They knew they were going home.

Fluffy snowflakes teased the sky when, in early afternoon, Roland glimpsed the banks of the Fox River. He turned onto the trail that took a northwesterly direction and, being a careful man, checked his direction with a compass. His fur-lined mittens caused him to bobble the instrument and it fell behind a box of Genevieve's china. *The hell with it,* he thought, *I'll get it later. Just keep the Fox River in sight and stay on the trail.*

Roland munched on a loaf of sourdough bread soaked in sorghum and placed it on the seat beside him. The weather was turning—the sky grew overcast and a north wind picked up. The team trotted well, keeping up a mile-eating pace. Fresh horse tracks peppered the trail, Roland noted. Later a horseman waved at him from the south. Must be near a settlement, Roland thought and the idea cheered him.

He passed a cabin and a mile later, came upon another. He stopped a stone's throw from the front door and helloed the house. A man in a bear coat came out on a rickety porch.

"Name's Johnson. How far you goin'?"

"Sharp's Point or thereabouts," Roland answered. "Where's the Bloomfield Settlement?"

"Go over the river and it's maybe ten miles south," Johnson said. "Going to snow like hell. Stay here all night. Only cost you a dollar. Gold," Johnson said.

"Never heard of paying for hospitality, Johnson," Roland said.

"Never met me before."

"No, I guess not," Roland snapped and flicked the reins.

A flurry of snow swept over them and plastered the trees that guarded the Fox. It left behind an ominous quiet. The sky was darkening. Roland noticed the birds and small game had disappeared. Ebb became irritable, tossing his head and snapping his teeth. *Ebb hates storms,* Roland thought. *We're bound to have one.* He said the Lord's Prayer out loud and clucked at the team.

The sledge had just come down from a ridge when the storm hit them. The trail just ahead of him became a swirling dervish of snow. Roland clucked at the team and snuggled in his buffalo hide. *It will be all right,* he told himself. *Go quarter-wise into the storm with the north wind on the right cheek–that keeps a body going northwest.*

The sledge evened itself and Roland knew they were on level ground. He slowed the team to a walk and looked ahead through frozen eyelashes. He sensed he had missed the trail. An upset sledge in this storm would be a disaster.

He pulled on Ebb's rein and steered the team a little more northwest. The land lay flat and the snow drifted around the horse's knees. The rasp of the sleigh's runners on the snow announced that the weather was getting colder. He reckoned it was about four o'clock in the afternoon and almost dark. A black smudge appeared ahead of him. Trees? Branches slapped the side of the sleigh. The horses started down a dip in the prairie and stopped. The doubletree smashed into the team and one horse grunted in pain.

Roland was catapulted out of the sledge and between the horses. Furious, he pulled himself up on Flow's rump and slid into belly deep snow besides the gelding. His feet skidded on a hard, smooth surface. Ice! Where could he possibly be? Confused, he scanned the area and noted several large cottonwood trees. A square box hung from one of them. A mail box, of course. With luck, he had struck the crossing at Soap Creek. He knew exactly where he was, still a long ways from home and his family a long ways from getting a full belly.

He grabbed the reins, and standing next to the sleigh, whooped at the mired horses. The tired team pulled the sledge a foot and stopped. Out of temper, Roland cracked his whip above the horses. Flow strained forward, but Ebb was faking. He laid the whip on Ebb two, three times. Both horses were on their bellies making serpentine motions, and slowly, almost imperceptibly, the loaded sledge inched up the other bank.

Once on level land, Roland walked to the front of the team. The animal's muscles quivered and great gouts of steam shot from their nostrils. "Ebb and Flow, don't you fret none. We're going to get through this. And when we get home, you'll get grain, hay, and three, four days rest—all of us." He patted Flow's neck, praised her, and then screamed with pain when Ebb bit him on the shoulder.

Roland drove the team at a fast walk, taking advantage of breaks in the driving snow to keep them on the ridges and out of drifts. Twice he smelled wood smoke and turned his team towards it only to lose the scent. He had no idea where the trail was and resolutely headed in a northwesterly direction. An eternity later, Roland realized he was traveling on a large expanse of flat ground. *Got to be due west of Moravia....only flat ground around here except for my place.*

The team floundered and stopped, mired in a drift. Roland stepped out of the sleigh and waded up to Flow. He grabbed onto his cheek piece and pulled the horse forward. A whoop and the team sloughed through the deep snow. Again, Roland smelled wood smoke. He hunched down, trying to see through the driving snow. A small cedar tree, uprooted by the wind, caromed across the prairie, and into the corner of Ebb's vision. The gelding bolted, dragging Flow with him. The team and loaded sledge disappeared into an opaque curtain of snow.

With a cry of despair, Roland raced after the team. His food, rifle, compass, and flint and steel were on the sledge! Roland ran until he hit the first snowdrift. The running man's momentum carried him deeper. He was immersed in snow. It became his entire world. There was no top or bottom. All he could do was make swimming-like motions. Somehow, he managed to get on his side. He discovered he could make progress by rolling.

He continued to roll. Snow fell down his neck into his mittens and boots. He rolled until the branches of a cedar brushed his face. Encouraged, he sat up and felt frozen buffalo grass. Desperately tired, and shivering from the wet cold, he forced himself to reason.

Our place is due north about six miles, he thought. *Just walk straight into the wind and stay on the ridges. Bound to hit Coal Creek. Get that close, a blind sow could lead me home.* Roland bent his head and trudged into the rising wind.

Twice he stopped to rest; the second time in the shelter of a bearded giant of a pine. He huddled there, arms at his side, trying for warmth. It was a pleasure to rest, and Roland felt an overwhelming desire to sleep. He nodded his head and dozed. The specter of his family hollow-eyed from hunger jerked him awake. Roland took a step and felt as if he were floating. He stamped his feet. Nothing.

Roland took off his boots and peeled away sodden wool socks. Ignoring the discomfort, he reached inside his coat and tore off the bottom half of his heavy shirt. He wrapped his feet in dry flannel and jammed the wet boots on again. He jumped up and down until his feet tingled. And Roland started into the wind again.

Head bent forward, the homesteader took long strides, staying on the ridges, and taking the full blast of the wind. He felt an uncontrollable anger at the storm that had taken his team and sledge, and now demanded his life. With aching legs and bellowing lungs he climbed another ridge, grabbing saplings to pull his way up in hip-deep snow. His stomach rumbled from hunger. A picture of his family formed in his mind. He knew the storm couldn't have him. Mindlessly he walked on, imprisoned in a white world of cold and aching muscles, propelled by a relentless will.

After a night of endless torture, anemic daylight seeped into Roland's world. He hadn't found a point of reference or crossed a stream. Slowly he accepted the fact that he had missed his landmarks and was somewhere northwest of his homestead. He trudged on, sometimes skirting a drift, sometimes bulling through it. The searing worry of his family became a mantle riding on his back. Time became a never-ending blur of alternate light and dark, and always, the blinding, driving snow. Roland plowed on, a resolute man against a man-killing storm. He was past hunger, past worry, only determined to beat the storm. But will power, sinew, and muscle can only take a man so far.

Roland reeled across a length of prairie blown clean of snow by an errant wind. He lunged forward, staggered and fell face down in the frozen grass. Suddenly it was warm and a treacherous sleep crept upon him. He placed a mittened hand on his face and curled into the fetal position.

"Roland! Roland, get up!"

A blue-cloaked man stood in front of him. He was tall and powerfully built, Roland discerned, seemingly unaffected by the storm. A luminous aura surrounded him. Roland smiled, and put his hand up when the man approached him.

"Come on, we've only got a short ways to go. I came here to help you," the man said and lifted Roland to his feet.

He made a motioning signal his hand and started across the prairie. Roland followed. He wasn't tired anymore. The wind hit Roland's left cheek. 'That's the wrong way," Roland croaked. "We want to go north."

The man ignored him. They walked in silence to a fringe of trees. The man was gone. Then he appeared to Roland's left in a frozen creek bed and waved Roland forward. When Roland was on the ice, he put his hand on Roland's shoulder and walked with him. Wood smoke! In the recesses of Roland's tired brain, the survival instinct triggered and Roland stared into the snow. Again, the pungent odor of smoke wafted past his nostrils. Hound-like, he picked up the scent and went towards it.

Around the next turn in the creek bed sat a cabin, perhaps fifty yards from the stream. Roland watched it as he shuffled forward on the ice. His tired eyes were out of focus. He tried not looking directly at the object and blinking rapidly. It was a cabin. He turned to tell that to the man who had saved him. His friend was gone.

Roland whooped and broke into a shambling run. A man and a woman, both dressed in buffalo robes came out the door. As he blurted his troubles in monosyllables, the couple each took an arm and helped him inside.

The scenes jumbled together like falling jackstraws mingled with hot soup and coffee, a warm fire, and finally, a blessed sleep.

The first time Roland woke, it was night. The next time it was the middle of the morning. The man had gone tending to his livestock, and the woman kneaded dough to rise by the fireplace. Roland got to his fee stiffly.

"Where am I, anyhow?" he asked.

"Not much of anywhere, mister. That there's the White Breast Crick out front. Maysville's a good twenty-five mile east on the trail—if you can find the trail, that is. Here, drink some coffee."

The woman gestured to a wooden box. Roland flopped down on it and stared at the steaming tin cup.

"What date is this?"

"Date? Let's see... I make it the eighteenth of January in the year of our Lord eighteen forty-five. Why?"

"I left Fort Madison on the twelfth. Should have been home on the thirteenth at the latest."

"Hee! Hee! You ain't home yet, neither! 'Nother storm could make up." The woman rocked back on the chair and reached in a frayed apron for her pipe. "You walked four, five days in that storm?"

"I guess so, made it anyway. Lady, I got to get home to my family!"

"Listen to me, mister. You leave now, you can make Maysville by dark and tomorrow take the trail south to Clark's Point. There's cabins every whipstitch on the trail. That's the safe way to do it," she told him.

Hurriedly he thanked the woman and made ready to go. She pressed meat and bread into his hands.

A brutal day's walk in the hip-deep snow brought Roland to Maysville just after full dark. Two bachelor brothers agreed to put him up for the night. Their log walls were poorly chinked and snow drifted onto the floor. The brothers assured him that the gaps were designed on purpose: "You see, the same snow that blows in one side is sure to

80

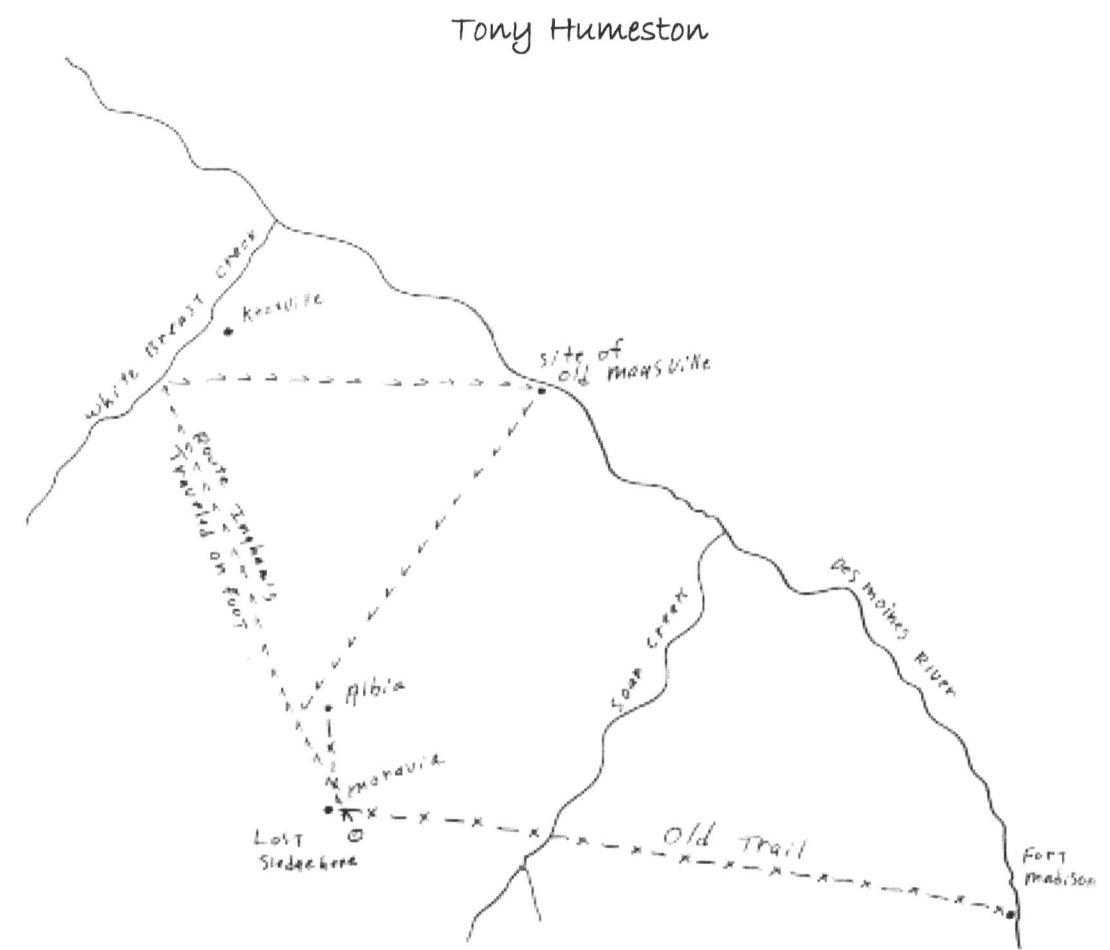

Sketch of the route which Roland Ingham walked from Fort Madison to his home near Albia.

blow out the other."

Roland thought a moment, smiled, and said he saw the logic in it. After a hot supper, he slept soundly in buffalo robes on the snow-covered cabin floor.

Dawn saw Roland walking south, towards Clark's Point. The crisp air smelled of snow and crackled under his feet. A cluster of stars blinked in the east. He followed the trail already broken by a rider on an unshod pony. A trio of wolves howled from a patch of timber a mile away and he watched a bay-colored one race across the prairie in a mile-eating stride.

The wolves reminded him of his team. He had seen what wolves did to horses. He pictured Ebb and Flow mired in the heavy snow and held captive in their harnesses. The wolf pack circling them, their baleful yellow eyes searching for a point of attack. By now, his team would be reduced to teeth gnawed bones and bits of hair, the supplies for his family, rifled and strewn over the prairie. Come green-up time, whoever found his sledge might send word to Genevieve.

The jingle of sleigh bells on an approaching sledge cheered him. He stepped out of the trail and waved. When the sledge pulled alongside, driver *whoa-ed* the team and gave him a hand up. The driver wore a bear coat and fur hat. His gray beard hung well below his chin, and the corners of his mouth were streaked with tobacco juice.

"Ain't you cold?" he asked.

"A man could say that and not be wrong," Roland answered.

"Here, take this." He handed Roland a buffalo robe. "My old woman heated a rock and wrapped it in a scrap of quilt." He slid a plaid object towards Roland. "Slip your boots off and plant your feet on that. Man with warm feet is warm all over."

"How far you going?" Roland asked.

"A pretty fair piece. I can take you down to Cedar Creek Bottoms."

Roland leaned back and luxuriated in the warmth. His thoughts turned to his wife and family. *Genevieve is worried sick by now,* he thought. *No, she's given me up for dead. The supplies are lost and there's not enough food to get by until spring. We'll have to depend upon the generosity of our neighbors. Wonder how long that will last?*

The team is gone. No two horses could get home in that storm. Without a team, I can't farm in the spring. I can't even haul my family back to Indiana. He steeled himself against the idea of asking his Indiana relations for money. *Can't ask them for anything. That's why I came out here in the first place. Poor Genevieve, she should have married our preacher—he sure was sweet on her, or maybe that James fellow. He was a steady man with a dandy farm.*

"Here's as far south as I'm going, Mister. Good luck on your way home." He reached over and shook Roland's hand. "Don't keep your worries to yourself, you'll live longer."

Roland smiled his thanks and hopped off the sledge. Ahead of him lay Cedar Creek and past the creek, a long, steep hill. Roland bowed his head and started into the hip-deep snow. A half hour later, he stood at the crest of the hill. His winded lungs ached and the long muscles in his thighs were a burning agony. The trail ahead of him was dotted with cabins. One cabin had a corral fastened to its south wall. Roland suspected the homesteader brought his team inside during cold weather. A man came out of the cabin and went to his horses.

"Hey, Mister! Two bits silver if you take me home," Roland shouted.

"Where's home?"

"South west of Clark's Point five, six miles."

"Take you to Clark's Point for two bits."

"Done."

Roland rode double to Clark's Point behind the homesteader. Roland's mind seethed with worry and guilt. At Clark's Point, he dismounted.

"No place colder than on top a horse in the winter," Roland opined and stamped his feet.

"That's why I'm going in for a drink. You want to come?"

Roland looked at the mellow lamp glow in the sod hut's window. Thought of the bite of whiskey in the back of his throat. Remembered the comforting warm glow – and remembered his family. He shook his head.

"I got to get home," Roland said and started to walk again.

"Come on, get back up here." the rider said and slipped his boot out of the left stirrup.

"Thanks, Mister, I was just about done in," Roland said and swung back onto the horse's rump.

"Figured you was."

When they stopped at his cabin, Roland took a long look at his homestead.

"Home," he breathed. 'You want to come in?"

"No, I got to go get that drink."

"Thanks," Roland said and swallowed.

Ignoring the latchstring, he burst through the door. Genevieve and the boys were playing on the floor in front of the fireplace.

Genevieve jumped to her feet, her features slack with surprise. A smile cracked Roland's frost-covered beard and he swayed from fatigue. They stared at each other a scant second and embraced.

"Papa! Papa!" the two boys shouted and each hugged one of his legs.

Mutely, Genevieve gestured for him to sit on a keg. Roland sat and a boy jumped up on each knee.

"What happened?" she asked excitedly. "I gave you up for dead." Her words continued in a rush, questions and sentences running together. Genevieve finally stopped for breath and wiped tears from her eyes.

"Here, let me get you some hot coffee." She poured the steaming liquid into a shiny white cup.

"Where did you get this cup?"

Genevieve smiled, showing her perfect teeth. "The team and sledge came home days ago. I looked out during a break in the blizzard and there they were, standing out in front."

"They got away from me down by Moravia," Roland said. "Then I got lost in the storm."

"Weren't you scared, Papa?" one of the boys asked.

Roland looked at his two sons and up at his wife. He thought of the mind-numbing cold, the hunger, and the exhaustion. "No, I always knew I'd get back. It sure was worth it."

Drive west of Albia on U.S. Highway 34. After crossing Coal Creek bridge, turn south and go up a gravel road. Go about a mile on the main road. On the left, you'll see what used to be called the State Farm. Roland Ingham cleared and farmed that ground. To my knowledge, there's nothing left, not even a trace of his passing.

DID THEY HANG THE WRONG MAN?

The heavy bullet smashed though the window, hummed across the room, and thudded into the log wall. Ian Goodpaster pulled his wife to the floor and motioned his son Joshua to get down before blowing out the oil lamp. He scuttled across the room, staying below the window, and snatched his Winchester carbine from its perch above the front door. The rifle's action snick-snacked as Ian levered a cartridge into the weapon's chamber. Flat against the wall, he slid next to the front window and risked a look. Nothing. Ian looked again and saw a cold November night, a sickle moon, and an empty rutted trail that ran in front of his cabin.

"Josh, go get your brother down from the loft. Then I want you to get the two girls and bring them into our bed," Ian said.

"Why would someone shoot at us?" asked Prudence Goodpaster.

"I'm not sure."

"Are you going out and see?"

"No. That's what they want me to do—open the door so they can shoot me full of holes," Ian said and went to the other window.

84

He heard the pitter-patter of bare feet across the puncheoned floor and Prudence's whisper. He thought of their daughters' sleep-filled eyes and whispered to God to keep them safe. Joshua was at his elbow, pulling on his shirt.

"What do I do, Pa?" he asked.

"You look out from the windows on that side of the cabin. I'll cover this side. You see any movement, sing out. Don't go to sleep on me, hear?" Ian ruffled his boy's hair.

"I won't," Josh said and left him.

Ian leaned back and thought, *I'll watch from this window and then go to the one by the front door.* He ripped a strip of cloth from his bandana and plugged the bullet hole in the glass pane beside his head. Went to the front window. Looked out. Nothing. *They're surely gone by now,* he told himself and leaned back against the log wall. Ian went to the back window. Heard Prudence settling down the two girls.

Tired of standing, Ian flopped down in a nearby chair and rubbed the ball of his thumb on the Winchester's walnut stock. Later, the Seth Thomas on the mantel tolled ten times. Two hours and more since the shooting. *Prudence always puts the girls to bed before eight. Surely, the shooter's gone by now...*

Ian leaned back in the chair, bone tired. Must have split a hundred rails today. The cold seemed to sap a man's energy. He yawned and shut his eyes. Hours later he woke with a twitch. The fire in the stove had gone out and the cabin was cold. Outside, the eastern sky turned pewter gray. The cedar trees that formed a windbreak were limned in the early light. Birds cheeped sleepily. The staunch Joshua stood against the other wall, peering out the window.

"Build up the fire, Josh. I'm going to take a look around." Ian spoke briskly to hide his embarrassment.

A cold November morning greeted him. Crowbait, his yellow cur farm dog, rose from his bed of mottled straw and shook himself. Ian knew it was safe. The dog would have scented a stranger and set up a ruckus fit to raise the dead.

Ian walked out to the road, his frozen breath streaming behind him. Horse tracks, frozen deep in the mud, pocked the trail. Ian read the sign. *Medium-sized horse carrying a heavy rider. Left front shoe has a corner broken off the outside edge. Hmm.*

From habit, Ian went to the corral. Crowbait hurried ahead of him, running through patches of brown grass and old snow. His horses looked jim dandy; they were clear-eyed and wearing healthy winter coats. The two brindle milk cows mooed from their stalls in the barn, begging to be milked. Ian knew he was late with his chores, but family came before livestock.

He scraped mud from his boots and turned toward the cabin. Inside his family was stirring. Prudence had located the lead slug in the wall and pointed to it. Ian dug the bullet out with his belt knife.

"Fifty caliber," he said and bounced it in his palm. "Did you hear its noise?"

"Yes, it hummed," Prudence answered.

"Spencer rifles make that sound. Gun sellers called them 'hummers' when they first came out. Then they called them 'humdingers.' Probably sold more rifles that way," Ian said.

"So what do we know for sure?" Prudence asked.

"For sure, we know a heavy man who owns a horse with a chipped front shoe and a Spencer rifle took a shot at us."

"What do we do now?" Prudence asked.

"Chris McAllister is going to drop by early on. Maybe he can help us figure this out," Ian said. "Let's have some breakfast."

"Pancakes coming right up!" Prudence smiled.

After breakfast, Ian sent Joshua do to do the milking and relaxed with a second cup of coffee. There wasn't much farm work to do this time of year except chores, clear land and split rails. Splitting rails could wait. This shooting business was more important. The cold realization hit him. He might have to kill the man who tried to hurt his family. But first, he had to be sure.

When Chris McAllister arrived, Ian told him what had happened and showed him the bullet.

"That's got to be Pleas Anderson," Chris said and rubbed his bare hands over the Round Oak heating stove in the middle of the room. "I had trouble with him over a pile of rails I'd split last summer. Always did think he took me on the deal."

"I had trouble with him over a bee tree the boys found and carved their name on. He claimed it," Ian said.

"Pa knocked him down twice and kicked him in the butt!" Malachi shouted.

"Malachi!" Prudence warned.

"Let's go see Pleas Anderson and see what he has to say," Ian said and reached for his coat.

"That suits me clear to the ground," Chris said. "Good morning, Missus Goodpaster, kids."

"Good morning to you, Mister McAllister. Tell Lois hello," Prudence said as they went out the door.

Pleas Anderson stopped driving nails into his corner post when they rode up. He set the hammer on the top rail and jammed his hands in his sheepliner. Anderson swaggered over to them, a confident man, well-pleased with himself. He tilted his hat brim back and flashed an insolent grin. Ian noticed his face was pitted when he looked up at them.

"Something I can do for you fellows?" Pleas asked.

"Yes. You can let me look at that sorrel gelding in your corral," Ian said and swung down.

"You want to buy him?" Anderson asked.

Ian slipped between the rails and waded through the mud to the gelding. The horse was skittish. Ian grabbed the halter's cheek piece and made soothing noises. In a moment, the horse settled and nuzzled Ian's coat. Ian raised the horse's left front leg and saw the damaged shoe.

"You went by my place last night, didn't you?' Ian demanded.

"What if I did?" Anderson asked.

"You own a fifty-caliber Spencer?"

"What if I do? What business is it of your'n?"

"I think you shot into my cabin last night. I just can't prove it. But I saw your horse tracks. That happens again, Anderson, and you're dead. No warning, no mercy, just dead," Ian shouted.

"Don't get yourself all het up, Ian. I rode past your cabin last night because it happens to be on the road to my place. It's muddy, so my horse left tracks," Pleas said.

"You hear what I said?" Ian grated and touched his revolver.

"Yeah, I hear you," Anderson said and gazed at something in the distance.

"All right, Chris. Let's go home," Ian said and swung into his saddle.

The next morning Sheriff Allen rapped on their front door. Joshua let him in. Prudence sat on the fireplace hearth and had just run a wood sliver into a fresh loaf of bread. Ian sat at the table, a steaming cup of coffee in his hand.

"Somebody killed Chris McAllister last night. Shot him down dead in his doorway," the sheriff said.

"Oh, my God!" Prudence said and clapped her hands to her cheeks.

"I helped that to happen," Ian muttered.

"How?" Allen demanded.

"Someone shot into my cabin with a fifty-caliber Spencer rifle. The shooter's horse had a chipped shoe on its off foreleg. Chris and I guessed Pleas Anderson did it and went to see him. The horse track matched. He wouldn't say if he has a Spencer or not. Told him I figured it was him, but I couldn't prove it," Ian said.

"That's all I need to arrest him. I'll get a half-dozen men to go with me and bring him in."

"I'll go with you," Ian said.

"No, you stay here." Allen made a halting gesture with his left hand. " We'll need you to testify. I can't have you being confagulated."

"Confagulated?" This from Prudence.

"Yes, ma'am. It's a legal term. Most folks don't understand it," Allen said.

"I would imagine not," Prudence remarked.

That afternoon Ian looked up from splitting rails and watched Tom Ross and his son Joe ride to him and stop.

"We got 'em both, Ian," Tom said.

"Both?"

"Yeah, we got his brother William, too. They're both in jail. Sheriff's scared to death the vigilantes will break them out and hang them. By God, they ought to, him killing Chris McAllister that way."

"Chris was well liked," Joe said.

"Sit a while. Pru's got coffee on, I know," Ian said.

"No thanks. Got to get home before dark," Tom said and shivered. "Damned if being on a horse isn't the coldest place in the world."

"You got that right," Ian said and watched them ride off.

*****

A week later, Ian sat at the table opening his mail. Prudence thumbed the pages on a new Montgomery Ward catalog she had just received. Ian got a letter from a sister out East and another from a company wanting to buy farms. Finally, he opened the one he had dreaded. The State of Iowa Courts had summoned him to appear as a witness in the trial of Pleas Anderson. A change of venue had resulted in the trial being held in

Oskaloosa on December 13, 1883.

"I'll need my Sunday suit packed," Ian said. "I've got to go to Oskaloosa."

"Oskaloosa? What in heaven's name for?" asked Prudence.

"A change of venue. After they let William Anderson go for lack of evidence, the folks in Urbana Township were mad as wet hornets. You remember that. We have a history for lynching here, too. So, they sent the trial and Pleas up to Oskaloosa. Want to keep him safe, I guess," Ian said.

"I'll get your things ready so you can leave in the morning. Oskaloosa's got to be forty miles from here," Prudence said.

*****

Ian returned from Oskaloosa a thoughtful man. He was the main witness against Pleas Anderson. A county-appointed lawyer convinced the jury to find Anderson not guilty. After all, the attorney argued, you can't hang a man for riding his horse on the open road, and most everyone around here has a gun. *Makes sense,* Ian concluded.

One of Chris' uncles, Obe McAllister, stood up and shouted, " We have a different judge in Urbana Township, Your Honor—he's called Judge Lynch. You're sure to meet him, Pleas." The judge broke his gavel hammering for order and fined Obe McAllister ten dollars for contempt of court.

Then going out of the courthouse, Pleas had sneered at Obe McAllister and elbowed him. Obe punched him in the face. Pleas sat on the stone steps of the Mahaska County Courthouse holding a bandana to his bleeding, broken nose. He mumbled swear words and promised to settle the score with Obe and Ian in ways they couldn't even guess. The Mahaska County sheriff came up and told the two of them to choose between going home or going to jail. They chose to go home.

Late that afternoon, Ian met Tom Ross on the Blakesburg Road. It had been a cold, all-day ride, and Ian was anxious to get home. Courtesy demanded that he stop and exchange news. Besides, Tom was riding a black three-year-old mare that was broke to ride and drive. The animal was a natural trotter pulling a buggy, and Ian coveted her.

"Well, Tom, the law let Pleas go—said they didn't have enough evidence and I think the jury was right. You can't hang a man for riding down the road," Ian said.

"No, you're wrong, Ian. Pleas needs his neck stretched. Do the whole county good," Ross said.

"Come on, those days are over," Ian said. His gelding tossed his head, mouthed the bit. The horse knew where he was and wanted to go home. Ian smiled and patted his neck.

"Ol' Pleas won't have much of a homecoming. His brother left the county while he still could and Pleas got his house burned down," Ross said.

"The hell you say!"

"His family got out safe and moved in with Pleas' father-in-law, Fielding Barnes," Ross said. "We can slip down there any night and get him."

"No, the law has spoken. Let's stay on our own farms with our families. Forget Pleas. I'm going home. See you, Tom," Ian said.

"See you."

Ian spurred his mount into a canter and rode towards his family.

Rumors flew about Pleas Anderson. He got in a fight in Blakesburg and kicked a man cross-eyed. One of the Stewarts had a horse hamstrung. Another neighbor came home from church and found his team stolen. Hiram Goodfellow had his barn burned.

In an effort to placate the farmers, the sheriff from Ottumwa rode out to Urbana Township and told anyone who would listen that Pleas couldn't have done those things—he was in jail at the time. Regardless, the Clayton brothers and Tom Ross were talking about a vigilante trial and lynching.

On the afternoon of December 29, Prudence came out to the barn. She was upset. Ian stopped forking hay and went to her.

"Ian, the kids came home from school upset. They met Pleas Anderson on the road. He nodded to them and continued about his business. The kids hadn't gone ten feet when Adam Clayton came out of the woods and took a shot at him. Pleas shot back and rode away. Adam told Josh to tell you the vigilantes will stop by for you before dark," she told him in a small voice.

A white rage seesawed through Ian. The scene flashed through his mind. Eliza and Sarah riding bareback on Peaches, the painted pony. Joshua and Malachi riding next to them on Pepper. All four scared to death. He speared a stack of hay with his fork and went to Prudence. He held her face in his rough hands and said, "I could beat Adam Clayton to a frazzle for endangering our kids. But you can't shoot a man for riding down the road. Pleas might be rougher than a cob, but there's no evidence linking him to any of this trouble—just his reputation. And part of that's hearsay."

"I fear for the children, Ian. We can't have this kind of trouble in Urbana Township," Prudence said.

In the cabin, he strapped on his gun belt and wolfed down a tepid supper. Without being told, Josh saddled his horse. Ian glanced from one child to the other: Eliza, Sarah,

Joshua, and Malachi. His faced flamed with anger and his eyes bulged like walnuts. He was waiting outside when the Clayton brothers and Tom Ross on horseback, with his two oldest sons in a sleigh, came by.

"You guys going after Pleas, ain't you?" Ian asked.

"We're going after Pleas Anderson. We figger to hang him," Seth Clayton said.

"I'll go with you, but damn it all, you can't hang a man for making horse tracks," Ian said and swivelled in his saddle. "As for you, Adam Clayton, shoot around my kids again and I'll wring your neck like a chicken's."

Ross made a soothing gesture with his open palms. "Cool down, Ian. Nobody got hurt. Come on with us. We'll get Pleas legal-like."

"We're going to nab him," Seth Clayton said. "Pleas and Fielding always goes out to the barn and feed his stock before supper. We can wait behind a stack of wood and get him."

"I've watched them for a couple nights—same routine every time," Adam Clayton said. "After we get Pleas, we're to take him to the Prairie School House—you know the one two miles east of Blakesburg?"

"Yeah. I'll go with you, but Pleas gets a fair trial," Ian said.

"Good enough—a fair trial first," Tom Ross remarked. "Hell, we haven't had a good lynching in this county for seventeen years. That's a quite a spell!"

"You are not going to have a lynching without a fair trial. Pleas Anderson has to be proven guilty," Ian said and fell in behind them.

They left their horses in a copse of woods several hundred yards from Barnes' homestead. Under the cover of darkness, the vigilantes crossed an open field and hid behind a pile of rails next to the barn. Soon Pleas Anderson and Fielding Barnes came out of their cabin. Barnes held a lantern in his hand and from the sound of their voices, the two were arguing. Ian watched the two men come closer and wondered why they couldn't sense something was wrong. He could have reached out and touched Pleas Anderson when three of the vigilantes stood up.

"We have guns on you both. Raise your hands up. Don't even make a twitch!" Tom Ross said.

"Whoa up, you guys," Barnes said. "Hold on. Let's talk about this."

"Barnes, this is not your look-out. You go to your house and stay there. Don't follow us or you're sure to die, " Adam Clayton said.

The vigilantes marched Anderson across Barnes' barnyard and into Ross' sleigh. 91

"You are going to take a little ride, Pleas, and have a trial," said Tom Ross.

"I'm innocent! Anyhow, you can't try me twice for the same crime," Anderson protested.

"Well, just watch us," the driver said and drove his team in the direction of Blakesburg.

*****

Ian whistled at the large crowd that stood in the schoolhouse yard. He swung out of the saddle, tied his horse on the hitching rail, stamped his numbed feet in the snow and felt them tingle. Tom Ross and Adam Clayton had Pleas's arms twisted high behind his back. They pushed through the crowd, forcing their way inside the schoolhouse. Ian followed in their wake and found a place to stand in the door. Beside him were two women. One whispered, "I hope they hang him. I had the croup and missed the last lynching." The other nodded and said something behind her hand.

Tom Ross had seated Pleas on the dunce's chair at the front of the room. Across the room from him were twelve men, some sitting on desks, the others lounging against the wall. Zach Sutton, a hard man but a fair one, stood between them. He leaned back on the schoolmarm's desk, and a leather holster showed at the edge of his coat. On the floor, in front of them, lay a heavy rope, one end fashioned in a hangman's noose.

Seth Clayton came in, and Ian watched him drape a quilt over his head. "Cover your head with this old quilt and come on with us. We're going to take him. The hell with a trial."

Ian shook his head and pushed Seth away. Three men, their heads all covered, followed Seth, staying between the school desks. At the front of the room, Seth faced Zach Sutton.

"We have come to take Pleas Anderson. We intend to hang him from that big cottonwood tree in front of Chris McAllister's cabin," Seth said from under his quilt and pointed his revolver at Sutton.

"Why don't you show your faces? Are you men cowards?" Zach Sutton demanded.

The one-room schoolhouse rocked with shouts and angry voices.

"Pleas is not guilty by a court of law!" Ian shouted and knew his voice was lost in the uproar.

"Just a minute," Sutton shouted. "We have to have a jury vote."

"No, sir! He's going to hang!" Seth Clayton shouted.

Sutton put up a restraining hand. "Jury—how do you vote?"

"HANG HIM!" they shouted in unison.

Sutton shook his head in disgust and stepped away. Seth Clayton slipped the noose around Pleas' neck.

The crowd cleared a path for Seth and the vigilantes as they hustled Pleas Anderson out of the schoolhouse. A hundred or more people had gathered outside, Ian guessed from his perch on the school steps. People mocked and cheered. Punches fell on Pleas, and once he staggered. The quilt covering Seth Clayton's face slipped down around his shoulders as he pulled on the rope that dragged Pleas Anderson. Strong, angry hands pushed Pleas down in the sleigh. Tom Ross's oldest son slapped the reins and the team started forward. Ian mounted his horse and galloped after the sleigh, hoping he could reason with Seth Clayton.

The sleigh stopped in front of Chris McAllister's cabin. The jutting limb of the cottonwood hung above them. The rope sailed over the limb, and three men stood Pleas up in the sleigh. The doomed man faced McAllister's front door. Ian looked about in helpless anger. The yard was full of sleighs, horses, and people bundled and hunched against the cold.

"You got anything to say—now's the time!" A man in a bearskin coat shouted.

"Let him have his last words," Tom Ross said.

Pleas swallowed several times and tried to speak. Finally, his words came out in a rush. "Jake, take my boots off."

Several men held Pleas, and Jake pulled off his boots. Someone in the crowd grabbed them and sailed them towards McAllister's house.

"Tell my wife to take care of the kids and keep the family together," Pleas said.

"Tell that to the McAllister widow!"

"Tell that to her kids!"

"Stop this thing right now, Ross, or I'll shoot you dead!" Ian yelled and drew his Colt.

Something hard jabbed Ian's back. Bristled whiskers brushed his face and a whiskey voice grated, "Holster your shooter and hush up. I aim to have Pleas' farm. Stay out of this or die!"

"Lift him up on the seat," Ross said. His voice trembled.

Adam and Seth Clayton helped Pleas up.

"You're hanging an innocent man!" Ian shouted. Tears streamed down his face.

"That you, Ian?" Pleas said.

"Yeah."

"Pray for me, Ian."

"I will, and so will my wife and kids."

The rope tightened above Pleas' head. Adam and Seth Clayton jumped off the sleigh. Someone whooped and the team went forward. Pleas kicked and died facing the doorway of the man he was supposed to have murdered. In the morning, the mail carrier found his frozen body hanging there.

Pleas Anderson's grave is in the Ormanville Cemetery south of Ottumwa. Eight men were charged in his murder. A Monroe County Grand Jury refused to indict them for lack of witnesses. An Urbana Township farmer reputedly confessed on his deathbed to the murder of Chris McAllister and complicity in the lynching of Anderson.

VIGILANTE JUSTICE

The lynching of Garrett Thompson is factual. The courtyard scene, the description of Thompson's death, and his wife taking Thompson's body are written history. My primary sources are history books, letters, and family lore passed from one generation to the next. Naturally, I don't know the exact words of the conversations.

Zechariah Sutton scanned the faces of the five men who sat in the dappled shade of his white oak trees. They clustered around the table-sized flat rock in his yard that had served as an outdoor meeting place since he had bought the homestead twenty years ago. Buck, his older brother, weaved and steadied himself. Buck smelled of apricot brandy, and Sutton suspected the others had been drinking, too.

Something is afoot to make these strait-laced men drink during the day, he thought.

"Zack," Buck said," we have to do something about this horse thieving. On the thirteenth, McFadden had a team stolen."

"Somebody held me up and robbed me of ninety dollars. He had a sack over his face with a hole cut for eyes so I couldn't see who he was, but he was an awful big man on a strange horse," Eli Woodruff said.

"The widow Taylor had a horse stolen, and Buchanan lost saddles and bridles," Axel Gilbert said.

"I had a wagon stole," Joe Bone said. "I'd know that wagon anywhere. Carved my name under the front seat, didn't I?"

"He surely did. I was there when he done it, " said John Miller. Miller was a small, dark man with glittering eyes. He had made sergeant in the Fifth Iowa cavalry, and Zach figured him as a good man.

"What do you fellows plan on doing?" Zach asked.

"Get it stopped," Buck said.

"Garrett Thompson is behind it. We know that—just can't prove it," Woodruff said. "He lives over west of Blakesburg on the Bluegrass Road. There's maybe four of them living in cabins and shacks. They don't farm but have plenty of money and nice horses. So there you are."

"What do you want me to do?" Zach asked.

"Well, Zach, you got more savvy being a cavalry captain in the war and got a lot of grit in your craw. We want you to run things and get this stealing stopped," Buck said.

"Boys, I'm way behind on my work here." He squinted in the sunlight at his wife, Ginny, heavy with child, hanging clothes on the line. "Where's this Thompson from?"

"Missouri. He was a Confederate guerilla during the war," John Miller said.

"Then John, you and Joe take the south road past Thompson's place and head down into Missouri. You shouldn't have to go very far. Whoever's got that new wagon is going to want to show it off. You find the wagon, you might get enough evidence to get Thompson arrested," Zach said.

Three days later Buck galloped his horse to Zach's homestead. He bailed off this horse and windmilled his arms to keep from falling. He raced up to their cabin and tripped on the porch steps. Ginny sat in a rocking chair, knitting and trying not to laugh. Zach stood up. His lips formed a question.

"Miller found Joe Bone's wagon down by Unionville. The man that sold it was Garrett Thompson, so they claim," Buck blurted.

"What happened then?" Zach asked.

"They went through some legal rigamarole, and now Sheriff Andrews has Thompson and four of his gang in jail. Colonel Johnson is going to have a pre—pre—pre—something or other hearing tonight. If Thompson is freed he's going to burn us all out, his missus is telling around," Buck said and stopped to take a breath.

"Burn us out, huh?" Zach said.

He went into his cabin and returned wearing a gun belt.

"I'm going to be gone maybe a day or two. When the boys come in from the fields, keep them close to the house until I'm back," Zach said.

He saw Ginny's eyes go to his gun belt. Worry masked her face.

"Do you have to do this?" Ginny asked.

"Yes. Don't worry."

"I shan't worry. I'll pray for you both," Ginny said.

By the time Zach and Buck got to town, there were a score of riders behind them. They stopped at the Grand Army of the Republic Hall and went in. Thompson and his cohorts sat on kegs facing the sheriff and Colonel Johnson, the town attorney. Zach's men weaved their way through the crowd until they were on the front row.

Sheriff Andrews stood up and raised his pistol. "Thompson, you and your men get to the back of the hall. We won't have a lynching in my county!"

A wave of Iowa homesteaders, their muscles hardened by years of drudgery, pressed forward. Their boots trampled on the wooden floor. Men cursed and shouted. Chairs were knocked down and a stack of hand-written notes tipped and fell underfoot. Colonel Johnson barked an order and was hurled against the wall.

"I'll shoot the first man who comes another foot closer!" the sheriff warned, waving his revolver.

"Put down your gun, Pete! You want to shoot a couple of good Republicans?" Buck Sutton demanded.

"I 'spect maybe you're right," he said and holstered his revolver.

The mob pushed past the sheriff and closed on the Thompson gang. Angry hands clutched the terrified men, twisting arms and propelling them across the room. Two of the suspects wrenched their way loose. An eddy of angry men grappled and heaved. The two men were slammed to the floor, kicked and beaten.

"I'm innocent!" Thompson shouted over the hubbub. "You are going to hang an innocent man!"

The vigilantes and their captives crammed through the door and burst onto the steps. One man stumbled and four or five men fell on him. They rose, cursing, and snatched at the prisoners.

"Steal my best bay, will you?" a bearded man shouted and punched Garrett Thompson full in the face.

The fifty-some vigilantes half-carried, half-dragged the terrified Thompson gang across the courtyard heading in a southeasterly direction. A short distance behind followed Sheriff Andrews with his impromptu posse. At the sheriff's orders, several bystanders joined him. The struggling captives slowed the vigilantes and the posse closed within arm's length. Insults were exchanged, and offers to single combat were tendered and accepted. One of the vigilantes, a harness maker named Calhoun, challenged Captain Mason. The two belligerents squared off in the courtyard and the posse stopped to watch the fight. The vigilantes marched the Thompson gang to an open tract of land north of the Doctor Gutch brick house where they had horses and wagons waiting.

*****

The next morning Zechariah Sutton pulled back the tent flap and stepped outside. It was early light and the men were rousing. They made the same hacks and snorts his cavalry command had emitted during the war. Eli Woodruff, his suspenders hanging about his knees, passed him heading for Avery Creek to wash. His brother Buck, suffering the ravages of a hangover, placed a coffee pot on a campfire ringed with stones. Zach remembered last night, turned, and counted the prisoners. They were all five there, hands tied behind their backs and lashed together like a daisy chain. Three sleepy-looking vigilantes carrying Springfield muskets guarded them.

John Miller was at his side with a steaming cup of coffee borrowed from someone else's fire. Zach accepted it with mumbled thanks and blew at the steaming liquid. *Miller is a good man and he must have made someone a hell of a good sergeant,* Zach thought.

"What's the plan, Cap'n?" Miller asked.

"Get five, six of our young men who are well mounted. Send them out in each direction for five miles. Have them spread the word we are going to try the Thompson gang at ten o'clock today for horse stealing, robbery, and anything else we can think of short of pissing on the road," Zach said.

"I'll take care of it, sir," Miller said and almost saluted.

Zach hid a smile and turned to the fire. Buck had bacon frying, and the aroma from a nearby Dutch oven signaled sour dough biscuits. *Better go wash up,* he thought and headed down the bank to the Avery Creek.

By nine o'clock the meadow next to the vigilante's camp started to fill with people. Families arrived by carriage and wagon. They spread quilts on the grass and placed picnic baskets on them. Barefoot boys wearing straw hats romped, and girls jumped rope or played jacks on the flat stones by the creek. Some of the curious strolled through the camp and looked at the prisoners with interest. Zach rubbed his boot sole in the grass and thought of things to do. He called for John Miller.

"John, find my brother Buck and put him in charge of rigging up a scrap of canvas as a screen latrine for the ladies. Tell Eli Woodruff to get five of our stoutest men and organize them into a peace committee. I mean, you tell them not to tolerate boisterous behavior or bad language. We are probably going to kill a man and that should not be taken lightly," Zach said.

"I'll take care of it," Miller said. "Hey Buck! Anybody seen Buck?"

"He's down by the crick," a pock-faced man volunteered.

"Go get him. Zach wants him right away." Miller said.

Zach looked at his pocket watch and said, "Time to get started."

John Miller brought Garrett Thompson, his hands tied behind his back, to face ten men who acted as jurors. Thompson's accusers testified, some tearfully, about what had been stolen from them. One farmer lost a team and missed a year's crop for lack of horses. Another had been robbed, and still another had his cabin shot into after stopping one of Thompson's men from stealing a prize colt.

It took the jury ten minutes to reach a verdict. Joshua Ames, a rotund man and the only juror wearing a business suit, whispered the decision to Zach. Zach nodded and faced the crowd.

"Garrett Thompson, it is the decision of this court and most everyone in Monroe County that you are guilty of horse stealing and probably did more things we don't know about. So, I hereby sentence you to death by hanging! Have you anything to say in your defense?"

"Yes. You-all sodbusters don't have enough wolf in you to hang me," Thompson said. He winked at the prisoners tied a stone's throw away, and they laughed.

"Uh-huh, you see that team and wagon under that limb over there?" Zach said and pointed to a large white oak. "That's where you are going, Thompson."

"Give him twenty minutes, Zach. He might think of something or make his peace with God," Joshua Ames said.

"All right. Twenty minutes," Zach said and looked at his watch. "I think I'm going to take walk down by the creek. I need some time alone."

A bevy of young girls were splashing in the creek water. They held their dresses up around their knees and sang a schoolyard chant about a blind goose and a calico cat. Zach smiled at them and hoped Ginny would have a girl this time. He walked at the water's edge around a bend and sat on a log. Time to pray, he thought and removed his hat. He ran his index finger around the groove etched in his forehead by his hat's brim and shut his eyes.

Prayer didn't come easy. Thompson deserved to hang, he was sure of that. It didn't matter much if it was by a court of law or Judge Lynch.

Dead's dead. Zach winced. He remembered the carnage at Shiloh. *Those farm boys, both blue and gray, didn't deserve to die, but you do, Garrett Thompson. You are a threat to my family and my way of life. I'll kill you as quick as I'd kill a rabid skunk.*

When Zach got back to the camp, Thompson was standing in the wagon box under the tree limb. John Miller was fashioning a hangman's noose from a length of rope. Thompson said something and laughed. Miller nodded and finished the knot. Another vigilante threw the rope end over the limb. A tall man in brown linsey clothes fastened the noose around Thompson's neck and placed a wooden box at his feet.

"What time is it?" Thompson asked.

"Eleven-twenty o'clock," someone answered.

"What do you care? You're not going anywhere—except to hell," Buck Sutton said.

"Give me until noon," Thompson said. "I've been thinking on some things."

"You've got until noon," Zach said. "You got anything to say for yourself, tell us now."

Thompson was silent. Time dragged by on leaden boots for Zach. He couldn't eat lunch and too much coffee had given him heartburn.

The crowd had swollen to at least five hundred, he reckoned. A woman and her teen-aged daughter were in a wagon away from the crowd. The woman's posture was rigid with anger. The younger one had a kerchief to her face. Must be Thompson's family, Zach mused. He went from group to group making small talk and checking his watch. The prisoners heckled him. Zach ignored them. Thompson remained silent.

At noon, Zach stepped over to the hanging tree. Buck marched the prisoners to where they faced Thompson at the foot of the wagon. In a loud voice, Henry Scott prayed, beseeching a merciful God to accept the soul of Garrett Thompson. The doomed man face turned ashen, and his eyes rolled with fear.

John Miller swung into the wagon with Thompson and said, "Step up on the box."

Thompson shook his head in refusal.

"G-d d-n you, get up there and die like a man!" Miller shouted over Scott's prayers.

Thompson stood still, his feet rooted in fear. Three men jumped into the wagon and lifted Thompson onto the box. Callused hands pulled the rope tight and snubbed the loose end off on a stob. The team lurched forward and Thompson swung free. A cluster of green caterpillars dropped onto his swinging body, and the crowd oohed and aahed. Zach thought he was going to get sick.

"You sons-a-bitches saw what happened to your boss. Do you want the same?" Zach asked.

The four trembled like palsy victims, spoke incoherently and shook their heads.

"Leave Monroe County and never return, or you can expect to be shot on sight," Zach said. "Understand? Buck, Miller, untie them and run them out of here, except for Buzz Thayer. Thayer, you stay here. You're going to stand trial," Zach said.

The rattle of wagon wheels distracted Zach. Garrett Thompson's wife drove a team beside her dead husband. "Can I have my old man now, Mister Sutton?"

"Yes, ma'am. Lower the body down and put him in Missus Thompson's wagon," Zach directed the vigilantes.

"May God curse you-all for murdering an innocent man! I'll be back and make you pay for this! I know every one of you bastards!" she screamed while they slid Garrett Thompson's body onto her wagon. "I'll make you pay and burn you out of your stinky cabins!"

"Come back to Monroe County, madam, and I promise you will receive the same fate as your husband. You are surely an accomplice to his crimes," Zach said. "Now leave!"

After Thompson's wagon was gone, Zach turned to Buzz Thayer.

"Go sit on that stump over there. The jury wants to question you."

"You tell your story same as you told me this morning, Buzz," one of the jurors said.

"I helped rustle four horses in Appanoose County. They were all sorrels. I put acid on their muzzles to turn their coats white and doctored up a bill of sale," Thayer said.

"Appanoose County, huh? Well, that's not so bad," a juror said.

"No, but it's horse stealing and we set up shop today to hang horse thieves."

"How did you get into this mess, Buzz? Now tell us the truth, or I'll hang you from that same limb we used on Thompson," Zach said.

"Garrett sold me a couple of horses real cheap. I sold them in Ottumwa and doubled my money. Then he told me I was dealing in stolen horses. I didn't know how to get out," Thayer said. "That was a couple years ago. But I never hurt anybody, never robbed anybody."

A man in the crowd wearing a black beard and blue overalls stood up. The chew in his cheek gave his face a misshapen look. "I served with Buzz Thayer in the Twenty-Second Iowa Infantry for three years. He got wounded twice. Buzz doesn't have the brains of a bullhead catfish, but he was a good soldier. That ought to account for something."

"Buzz Thayer and good sense were never on speaking terms," Buck said in a loud voice and everyone laughed.

A woman in a calico dress and a blue sunbonnet stood up and said, " Zach Sutton, everybody knows you are hard as nails and straight as a rifle barrel. Buzz Thayer is probably guilty of more than he is telling us. But it's time to temper justice with mercy. Let Mister Thayer go."

"What do you think, boys?" Zach asked and turned to the jury.

"Hang him!" a whiskey-faced man in the front row shouted.

"No! I'm not voting to hang a wounded veteran," another said.

Two jurors, both drunk, stood and swung at each other. They stumbled, clutched at each other's clothes and fell to the ground. The other jurors stepped back, making room for the fighters.

"Let's vote! Everybody for letting Buzz go, raise your hands! The two wallowing on the ground count one for, one against," Zach said. He counted hands and turned to Thayer.

"Buzz, you squeaked by six to four. You're a free man. Don't get in any more trouble," Zach said.

Two more jurors, Bob Brooks and Jethro Summers, exchanged insults. Brooks punched Summers in the face and cousins from both sides jumped in. A dozen men cursed, pummeled each other, and rolled on the ground.

"Buck, let's get our horses and go home," Zach said.

They walked through the grove and swung into the saddle.

"Justice has been served. Well, sort of," Buck said.

"Sort of," Zach said and pointed his bay in the direction of his homestead.

BEN GUNNION'S LOST GOLD

I came across the story of Ben Gunnion in an old newspaper clipping a friend gave me. Ben Gunnion's murder actually happened in Mahaska County. But Mahaska is close to Monroe and one of the murderers did flee to Albia. Anyhow, as thin as it is, that's my reason for including the story.

By all accounts, Ben Gunnion was a solid citizen traveling from Illinois to an unknown destination in Iowa. He drove a team and wagon, and he had five thousand dollars in gold coin. Ben met two men in Ottumwa and offered them a ride. That night, they camped west of the Eddyville Cemetery about half way down the hill, on the trail, where the pavement is now. Folks say that stretch of concrete is the first pavement in the state. That night the two men got drunk and killed Ben Gunnion with an axe—actually chopped off his head.

In the killer's drunkenness, the gold was lost except for a few coins. Gunnion's skull was found the next spring at the campsite. His wagon showed up in a farmer's barnyard. One of the murderers was killed by a lawman. The other, perpetually drunk and haunted by the specter of Gunnion's head, told the story to whoever would listen to him. Eventually he hanged himself.

People that look up and down the road for the gold have found a few coins. Folks used to say that some nights Ben Gunnion is out and about looking for his head, so be careful out there.

Ben Gunnion should have known he made a mistake when he took payment of five thousand dollars in gold coin for his Illinois farm. But Ben didn't trust banks, and the bankers in Canfield couldn't convince him how anyone could send a wire transfer of funds from Springfield to Chicago and on to Council Bluffs, Iowa. Another thing, people talk, and he didn't want folks knowing his sweet Annie Burdock was out there in a boarding house waiting for him. Why, the Burdock brothers would bring her back quick as a knife.

Annie's family didn't want the Gunnions marrying in with them. Old man Burdock made that plain enough when Ben went to him and asked for her hand. The bearded old farmer shook his head and said, "Wrong religion—now git!"

Ben told the family patriarch that the traveling preacher who'd converted the Burdocks was a fraud. Shucks, anybody could drink colored water out of a bottle marked LYE and claim the poison didn't hurt him. Same thing with the rattlesnakes. That wild-eyed preacher man shoved his bare hand in a basket of snakes and brought it out clean. But nobody looked in the basket. It could have been full of garter snakes for all anybody knew.

But religion aside, he and Annie talked about how much they loved each other, and what were they going to do? Ben's cousin Jamie, who farmed outside of Omaha, wrote him that there was good farm land on the Missouri River bottoms a man could buy right. Ben talked to Annie about sneaking out there and they made plans. One night when everyone was at a Halloween party, Annie slipped away. Ben drove her to Springfield and bought her a one-way ticket on the train to Council Bluffs, Iowa.

Ben sold his farm to a neighbor. Both buyer and seller agreed to keep it quiet. Ben surrendered possession after the corn was picked and sent to market. He figured the Burdock boys to have an eye on him. In the cover of his barn, Ben painted his wagon blue and the wheels yellow in the fashion of folks moving west. As an afterthought, he smeared nitric acid on the muzzles of his matched sorrel team, Ginger and Snap. The acid worked as a permanent dye, searing a blaze of white on the team's faces. With the wagon color changed, and the horses's markings permanently altered, Ben knew he would just be one more anonymous homesteader in that endless caravan moving west. Only thing left to do was leave a false trail. Ben left a note in the barn, telling the new owner to hold his mail and that he would send for it when he got settled in Penfield, Indiana. After dark, Ben loaded his wagon with his personal belongings, hitched up his team, and headed west.

The windy November air chilled him, but the thought of Annie waiting in Council Bluffs steeled his resolve. He had five thousand dollars gold coin in a Bible box under the wagon seat. Close to hand rested a brand new Navy Colt six-shooter, primed and capped, the hammer resting on an empty chamber. Behind the seat, he had an Eli Whitney musket a family member had brought back from a now-forgotten war. That piece he kept unloaded. The mule-ear hammer on the weapon was an open invitation for an accident.

By mid-morning, Ben hooked up with a line of wagons bound for Oregon or California or wherever struck their fancy. They seemed to be from one area in Vermont and were abrupt, sharp-tongued people, not like the Midwesterners Ben had grown up around – the kind who took ten minutes of talking before getting around to telling you what they wanted. He chalked their brusqueness down as bad manners and decided to give them short shrift. Besides, he didn't have a cover story thought up. Lying wasn't his style.

After several days of traveling west, Ben saw two of the Burdocks brothers. They had stopped at a campfire a stone's throw away and were talking to a trio of Vermonters. Ben went to his team and fiddled with their halters, watching the Burdocks from under his hat brim. His heart was a hollow drum pounding in his chest. The Vermonters shook their heads and shrugged at the brother's questions. One of them, a burly man named Mike, glanced at Ben. His eyes slid over Ben's outfit and turned away. Ben watched them canter their horses back towards home. Ben figured he was safe.

Two days later, his team topped a rise and Ben got his first look at the Mississippi River Valley. Ahead of him sprawled a flat expanse of trees and a scattering of cabins. In the middle distance flowed a broad gleam of silver that was the largest river Ben had ever seen. Across the river, on the far shore, bristled a fringe of trees and some wooden buildings: Iowa.

By mid-afternoon, it was time for Ben and his team and wagon to load on the flat boat. Ginger started down the ramp but Snap would have none of it. Uncharacteristically Snap balked and tried to rear as much as his heavy forequarters would let him. Ben loved the horses and loathed whipping them. Leading wouldn't work; the bargeman tried that. One of the Vermonters tied scarves around both horses' eyes and led them onto the barge. Ben grinned his thanks. The Vermonter said, "Ye're a good fellow, lad!" and went back to his wagon.

Once again on dry land, Ben bent his head in a prayer of thanks. He swung down from the wagon box and went to his team. He untied the rags and rubbed both their muzzles.

"Ginger and Snap, I promise to never, ever, take you out on a big river like that again. I know you were scared from the way you tramped the floor. But you wasn't no more scared than I was," he told them.

Ben took the scarves back to the Vermonter and thanked him.

"Ye be careful, lad. My missus claims you are star struck," he said.

"Star struck?" Ben asked.

"Aye, she claims you will come to a bad end—though not by your fault." The New Englander chewed on his pipe stem and looked away. "Better watch your step."

"I will," Ben assured him and thought of his gold and the Navy Colt beside it. "I have to be careful."

Ben's introduction to Iowa dispelled the somber mood cast by the Vermonter. He had evaded the Burdocks. The haughty Vermonters had chosen some other route. The countryside was hillier than the mind-numbing flatness of Illinois. People were friendlier, but always working, always in a hurry—hard at it from light to dark.

He stopped the first night in New London and stabled Ginger and Snap. The painted sign of a bathhouse beckoned from across the muddy street. Ben picked his way between water-filled ruts and piles of fresh manure. He luxuriated in a warm bath and changed his clothes. A dime bought him a home-cooked meal in a boarding house.

The next day on the road the wind grew sharper. Ben figured it was well into the second week in November. Ginger's and Snap's coats were heavier. The wagon rolled westward, the horses pulling steadily. That night he stopped in Mount Pleasant. In the morning, Ben discovered that frigid weather froze the mud road iron-hard. The going was easy, and the team made Fairfield by nightfall. The next day he rolled through Agency and camped that night with a group of teamsters a few miles east of Ottumwa.

"Hey, Mister," someone said behind him.

Ben looked up from snapping the tugs on the doubletree. In the morning sunlight, he saw the bearded faces of two men.

"What can I do for you?" Ben asked.

"Looking for a ride west. We went off the payroll last night. Job's done," the nearest one said.

"Yep, I'll give you a lift. Take you as far as Albia, that help any?" Ben asked. The Vermonters words edged into his memory. His brushed the feelings away and grinned.

"Albia's fine," one of them said.

"Name's Ben Gunnion," Ben said and extended his hand.

"I'm Aaron Spires and this here is Hobe Jackson," Spires said. The men shook hands.

"Climb up," Ben said, put his foot in a wagon spoke and swung up onto his seat. Directly under him rested the gold, with the Navy Colt beside it, handy and within reach.

The Des Moines River was bank full at Ottumwa. Ben drove down town and looked in awe at the tall brick buildings. The ferry was shut down after being rammed by a sawyer. A man in a fancy suit told him to head west on the river road: "There's a safe ford at Eddy's Post which some folks nowadays call Eddyville."

Ben said his thanks and pointed Ginger and Snap west.

Aaron Spires and Ben sat in the front seat and talked. Spires was a slippery man; the kind that holds a person's eyes a shade too long to prove sincerity. Spires fawned over Ben, complimented him. Ben told Spires his life story from the death of his parents and his inheriting the farm, to his romance with Annie. Told him how he tricked the Burdock brothers and sold his farm for top dollar. Later when Spires asked him if he trusted banks, Ben told him no.

They topped a hill and looked down on the city of Eddyville through falling snow. From the distance, the coal lamps burning in cabin windows appeared to be miniature fireflies. The three of them camped on a level place partway down the hill. There was a ring of fire-blackened stones and a windfall lay nearby. Hobe took an axe and went to cut firewood. Ben tended to his team while Spires dug food out of a gunnysack.

Once the victuals were done, they settled by a campfire and shared stories. Spires produced a quart bottle of whiskey and offered Ben a drink. Ben shook his head. Said he didn't hold with drinking or card playing. Spires and Hobe shared the bottle. After an hour's drinking, the conversation turned mean. Spires worked an argument out of the placid Ben.

Ben wished with all his being that he was alone. The man named Hobe was drunk, almost passed out leaning into the fire. Spires stood up reeling and pointed an index finger at Ben. Things were shaping up to a fistfight. Ben was confident he could handle the two without his Colt. His quickness and physical strength had been legendary around Canfield.

Spires, on his third try, go to his feet. He said something about getting firewood and stumbled behind Ben.

Spires picked up the axe leaning against the wagon wheel. The sharpened axe blade gleamed in the firelight when he swung it with both hands. The blade bit into the back of Ben's neck. Ben collapsed beside the fire. Spires stepped over the firestones and chopped down at Ben hitting him again and again. Chuckling he picked up a bloody object and thrust it between Hobe's knees. Spires settled down on a log and took a drink of whiskey.

"Hey, Hobe! Wake up!" he shouted.

Hobe roused himself, looked down at the sightless eyes of Ben Gunnion and shrieked. The blood-splattered Spires laughed until his sides ached.

Later, when Hobe had composed himself, the two decided to look for the gold. With lantern light and liberal infusions of whiskey, they climbed into the wagon. The two ignored the walking plow and hand tools carefully secured in the wagon's rear. A walnut bureau was the first likely spot to hide something Drawers were yanked out and clothes tossed aside. Two locked chests were broken into. More clothes, some papers, no gold.

Spires cursed and jumped off the wagon. He staggered to Ben's headless corpse and knelt beside it. Ben's sheepliner pockets held a Bible. Spires glanced at it, smirked, and threw it in the fire. The burning pages flared up. The nearby whiskey bottle beckoned. Hobe sat – or fell – down beside him.

Spires woke when dawn's light stole into the camp. He was cold. The fire had gone out. An arm's length away, Hobe slept on a stone, his body bent forward at an impossible angle. Spires stood up. Ben Gunnion lay at his feet. Pieces of last night came back to him. *The gold! Must find the gold before Hobe wakes up.*

Something heavy bounced in his coat pocket. He touched the curved handle of Ben's Navy Colt. The oiled weapon felt snug in his hand. Light caromed from the brass percussion caps attached to the cylinder's nipples. Loaded and set to go, Spires thought and pointed the Colt at the sleeping Hobe. *No. I can use Hobe.*

Spires's other coat pocket contained a dozen gold coins. *Now where's the gold? I surely found it or I wouldn't have this money.* Visions of gold coins gleaming in the firelight and wild laughter tumbled through his alcohol-fogged memory. He kicked at a lidless Bible box that lay at his feet. *Think,* he told himself. *We had the gold and we likely hid it. Where? We got too drunk and can't remember.*

Spires wracked his brain and scanned the camp area. The gnarled limbs of the undergrowth limned by a soft-falling snow seemed to mock him. He shook Hobe awake. Stood him on his feet. His breath made Spires turn his head. Hobe couldn't remember where they hid the gold. But he too, had a dozen gold coins.

Disgusted, Spires pushed him against the front wagon wheel. In the distance sounded the rhythmic chunk of someone chopping wood.

It was full morning and people were on the move. A wagon could come over the hill anytime. Spires considered his bloody clothes and the headless corpse of Ben Gunnion. No explanation he and Hobe could offer would hold up. They would be found guilty of murder and hung within a week. Time to go. They could always come back and find the gold later.

The men each grabbed a wrist and dragged Ben Gunnion into the woods a short distance. Hobe tossed an armload of tree limbs on him. They both almost ran back to the camp. In a heartbeat, the team was harnessed and hitched to the wagon. At the last minute, Hobe remembered the camp axe and slipped it behind the seat. Spires swung up into the box seat and heard the pocketed Navy thump against the wagon box.

Hobe doesn't know I have the gun, he thought. *That's good. A smart man always keeps the edge.*

Hobe swung up next to him and sat down with a grunt. Spires smirked and flipped the reins. Ginger and Snap started down the steep hill towards Eddyville.

Spires used the hand brake to keep the wagon from crowding the team. Even so, the descent was tricky. The frozen clay had become glass-slick under the fresh snow. The iron-bound wooden wheels slid, on the verge of crowding the team with the doubletree. Spires kept a tight rein, hoping to keep the horses under control. At the bottom of the hill, the trail intersected with a north-south track. A hand painted sign said "Oskiloosi 9 miles," and an arrow pointed north.

Hobe grunted in assent as Spires turned the team north towards Oskaloosa. Misplacing the gold ragged at Spires. But he had been drunk before and remembered things days later. The memory would come back, it always did. Sometimes a man just has to wait.

But he aimed to have the gold and not share it with that fool, Hobe. Spires touched the revolver's walnut handle. He could kill Hobe anytime. *The damned fat fool trusts people. Big mistake, Hobe. A feller has to get up pretty early in the morning to get*

107

ahead of Aaron Spires.

A few miles south of Oskaloosa, Aaron decided to sell Gunnison's outfit. He explained to Hobe that the wagon and team should bring a pretty penny and they'd rather ride horses. Suppose their luck turned sour and someone found Gunnison's body. Two shabbily-dressed strangers riding in a first-class wagon pulled by a good team could draw unwanted attention. Two men on horseback wouldn't even raise an eyebrow. Hobe sipped on the leftover whiskey and agreed.

The first two farmers said no deal. One wasn't interested and the other said he didn't have any money. Spires told Hobe all these Dutchmen had money, and for a frog hair, he'd come back here sometime and rob them, kill them, and burn them out.

The third one seemed interested. His name was Van Grooten. He had direct blue eyes and a shock of yellow hair that peeked out from under his fur hat. The farmer was an older man and a lifetime of pushing a walking plow had humped his back and lamed him. He limped around the wagon, climbed inside of it and then examined the team. Spires and Hobe kicked clods and corncobs and waited for his offer.

Spires admitted the two of them didn't have any papers on the team or the wagon. That appeared to be a deal-breaker until Hobe blurted out that they needed two good horses. Van Grooten cupped his hand and yelled something in Dutch. Minutes later, a boy led a pair of horses out of the barn; one was a gray, the other a black. Four-year-olds, Spires guessed. At Van Grooten's instructions, the boy mounted one and then the other and rode them around the barnyard, guiding them with a halter rope.

Spires and Hobe liked the horses. Van Grooten threw in saddle and bridles. Spires asked for boot. The Dutchman told him he had no papers on the saddle horses and they had no papers on the team and wagon. No boot. One hand washes the other. Take it or leave it. Spires touched the revolver handle. For an instant he envisioned Van Grooten and his boy writhing in the barnyard, gut shot. Spires choked down his rage and smiled at the Dutchman. Spires and Hobe took the deal. The two mounted men rode north towards Oskaloosa.

"This town is a nice place," Spires told Hobe. Hobe nodded and dismounted, tying his horse to a wooden hitching rack. Spires figured he needed a new suit of clothes and pointed to a clothing store. Hobe nodded and said he'd go have a drink in the saloon across the street. Spires clapped Hobe on the back and said when he came back they would go have a meal somewhere. "Looks like we got out of our trouble scot-free."

Half an hour later, Spires came out of the clothing store. He was shaved and bathed, wearing new linsey wool trousers and a cotton shirt and brocaded vest under his overcoat. Spires congratulated himself. His hangover was gone. He remembered where they had put the gold. So simple, he should have thought of it in the first place.

Need to keep an eye on Hobe. First chance he got, Hobe was dead. No sense sharing the gold. *Yes siree, things work out for a man who keeps his wits about him and watches out for the main chance.*

Van Grooten and a beanpole skinny man stood on the board sidewalk besides Spires' new horse. Perplexed, Spires walked towards them giving them his best smile and leaving his coat open in front so they could see his new clothes.

"That's the man, sheriff! Him and another feller stole these two horses from me. I got the titles to prove ownership right here." VanGrooten waved two pages of white paper in the air.

The thin man turned, and Spires saw a silver star on his coat. Spires plunged his hand in his coat pocket, fumbling for his Colt. His fingers grasped the handle of the weapon but the hammer snagged on his coat lining. Spires heard a cracking noise and a horrific blow struck his chest. He tugged again at the Colt and another blow hammered him. *My fancy vest is ruined,* Spires thought and fell forward on his face.

Across the street, Hobe Jackson heard the shots and looked out the dust-streaked window. Spires lay on the board sidewalk, two holes in him. The Dutchman was standing there with the sheriff next to their horses.

For a rare instant Hobe saw everything with sharp mental clarity. *Escape. Don't get seen, don't get caught.* With as much calmness he could muster, Hobe bought a bottle of whiskey for two dollars and strolled out the back door. A caravan of big Murphy wagons were wending south, and one had stopped outside the stoop. Hobe shinnied over the tailgate and landed on a pile of straw. A thought crept across his mind. *Those wagons are going south past Van Grooten's place. That's the last direction they would expect me to go.*

He snuggled down in the straw and took a hard pull on the whiskey. Hobe was asleep when the wagon started to roll.

Hobe sensed it was mid-afternoon when he woke. The hangover was gone, his mind clear. His stomach growled from hunger, but he had been hungry before. Hobe raised his head over the tailgate. It had stopped snowing. The land was hilly, and at irregular intervals, neat log cabins with smoke curling from the chimneys lined the rutted trail. Hobe watched the countryside roll past until unbidden memories of Ben Gunnion's sightless eyes and severed head skewered his conscience. Hobe looked heavenward and tried to remember a prayer. None came. He drank two inches out of the bottle and passed out on the straw.

His own screams woke him. Ben Gunnion's head floated through his alcohol-ridden mind. Frightened, he jumped down from the wagon. It was dark. A chilling north wind carried a slice of piano music. Ben saw window lights and staggered towards them. A passer-by told him that the tavern straight ahead served meals. Inside Hobe sat at a table and realized he was shaking like a man with palsy. He ordered whiskey and used both hands to grasp the brimming shot glass. With a smooth motion, he raised both forearms and drank the whiskey. The second shot went down, did acrobatics in his stomach and settled him. Hobe ordered a third shot before his meal.

The steak was tough and the potatoes cold. He slapped a five-dollar gold piece on the table and elbowed his way into a space at the bar. A bearded teamster next to him shouted that anyone who smelled like a goat should buy drinks for the house. Hobe laughed and threw the rest of his gold coins on the bar. The bartender, a huge man with a black handlebar moustache, slipped some of Hobe's coins into his apron pocket and poured drinks. Men clapped him on the shoulder. His world became a swirl of whiskey and animated people. Hobe squinted a peek into the mirror behind the bar, and Ben Gunnion's face leered back at him.

He shrieked in terror and burst out the door. Men, singly and in pairs, walked the boarded sidewalks of Albia. One of them could be Ben Gunnion. Hobe yelled his head was in the bar and pointed at the bat-wing doors. A passer-by glanced at Hobe and hurried away. Hobe ran down the sidewalk in mortal fear. At the corner, he stumbled and fell into the street. Back on his feet, he wiped blood from his forehead and ran on, through the open door of a livery stable.

Ben Gunnion was with him now, telling him what to do. Hobe threw a length of rope over a rafter and fashioned the end into a noose. He climbed the side of a horse stall and lashed the other end of the rope to a post. Gunnion was shouting at him now, telling him to hurry. He slipped the noose over his head and tightened the knot. A dozen Ben Gunnion faces jeered at him. Hobe jumped and heard a ping! in his neck as clear as a church bell on a Sunday winter morning. Then Spires was with him and they were falling, mouths open and empty hands clawing. Far below, a being emerged from a shadow, and Hobe saw something he had long ago told himself didn't exist.

DON'T MESS WITH HITEMAN

This is a straightforward account of some Monroe County lawmen and citizens who did their job in a matter-of-fact way. A threat faced the citizenry and Sheriff Goodwin took care of it: no braggadocio, no preening, no strutting. All he said afterwards was he couldn't have done it without some good help. Go west on the Hiteman Road about a quarter of a mile. You'll see a deep bank off to the south. That's where the robber's stolen car upset that April day in 1935.

110

The four Chicagoans waited an hour for the owner of the 1935 Oldsmobile sedan to leave the restaurant. The prospect of oncoming action animated them. The men smoked incessantly, alternately lowering and raising the windows of the driver's Model A Ford to dispel cigarette smoke and keep out the frigid Lake Michigan air.

They had spotted Doctor Higgins and watched his movements for a week. His habits never varied; the good doctor arrived at the Top Hat at eight o'clock, had two drinks, and ordered a large steak. At nine thirty, he lit a large cigar, paid for his dinner, and strolled back to his shiny-new car. "It must be nice, having money," the driver of the Model A said in envious tones. "Eat in a fancy joint like the Top Hat and tool on home in a new car."

A pock-faced man in the back seat opened his pocket watch and squinted at it in the dim light from the street lamp. "Should be coming out any minute now," he muttered and lit another Camel.

"That's him!" someone said from the front seat and got out of the Ford, a .45 Colt held low against his side.

He strolled towards Doctor Higgins at a leisurely pace, a man out for a stroll, going nowhere in general. The two men met besides the Olds. They stopped and talked briefly. Doctor Higgins handed over his keys. Head down, he hurried across the avenue and ran pell-mell down a darkened street away from the Top Hat and his shiny new Oldsmobile.

The driver whooped and started his Ford. He drove ahead and pulled into the curb behind the Olds. Two of the men jumped into their new car and followed the Model A to a house in Cicero. In an attached garage, they installed Iowa plates on the Olds and put three sawed-off Winchester '97 shotguns and a Thompson sub-machine gun in the back seat. All the men carried side arms.

A half-drunk woman stumbled into the garage and leaned against the car. She gazed at the four men with a familiarity that spoke volumes.

"Can't you wait another day? Tomorrow's Joey's birthday. You know how he loves you guys. Please, do it for me," she said.

"Tomorrow's Smokey Hollow payday. We can't wait another month, Kate."

"Can't you just do this for me? For me and Joey?" she implored.

"No. Get the hell out of the road," one of them said and slammed her against the garage wall.

"Ow! You hurt me, damn you!" Kate screamed and grabbed her shoulder.

A tall man turned from the open car door and backhanded Kate across the mouth. A horsetail of blood and saliva splattered on the garage wall.

"A woman has to know when to keep her mouth shut," he said. "Maybe that knuckle sandwich will help."

Kate took a piece of enamel from her tongue. "You busted out my front tooth, you bastard! You'll pay for that!"

"See you tomorrow afternoon, Kate!" Marvine's voice was laced with laughter and scorn.

The four bailed into the Olds and the driver backed the car out of the garage. All were in high sprits, anticipating easy money.

The men had discovered that robberies were much more lucrative than slaving in a sweatshop for Depression-era wages. They had morphed into a cohesive unit, working together and trusting each other as much as thieves can.

By this time in their criminal careers, the gang was seasoned pros. Ned Warner, 22, had been arrested for robbery and released for lack of evidence. George Schindler, 20, had been arrested for robbery and released. Mike Barra, 35, had no police record. James Marvine, 40, was a fugitive from justice. He had escaped from a New York penitentiary where he had been serving a fifteen-year sentence for robbery

Ned Warner wheeled the Olds left onto the main thoroughfare and drove south in the darkness towards Illinois Highway 6. They were on their way to Iowa. It was eleven o'clock.

At eleven-fifteen, Sheriff John Goodwin heard the telephone ring in the Monroe County jail at Albia, Iowa. Careful not to wake his wife, he tiptoed across the bedroom floor and raised the receiver. What he heard next jolted him awake.

The lisping female voice at the other end of the line told him the Smoky Hollow Mine payroll was going to be robbed tomorrow. The sheriff was skeptical and pressed for details. The woman said this gang was the same one that held up the mine payroll in Pershing. Goodwin grabbed a nearby pencil and paper and took down the information: Four men—armed and dangerous. Driving a shiny black Oldsmobile. On the Hiteman Road. A simple heist—just stop the bank car and take the payroll money.

The line went dead. Goodwin clicked the hook until he raised Central, only to find there was no way to trace a telephone call to Illinois.

"My God," Goodwin exploded. "This is 1935 and modern times! You mean you can't tell me where a phone call is coming from?"

"No sheriff. Not now, probably not ever," Central replied and clicked off.

Behind him, his wife padded across the linoleum floor in her house slippers to the kitchen. He heard water running in the sink. *Good, the missus is going to make coffee.*

Goodwin lit a cigarette and told Central to ring Assistant Chief of Police Ludwig Johnson's telephone number. He told Lud to get Deputy Sheriff Bill Frew and come to the jail quick. He called his friend Sheriff Grandman of Marion County and explained the situation. Grandman said he would be right down and bring Andy Lubberden with him. "Andy is a good man to have around when there's trouble," Grandman said.

Godwin sipped on some coffee and lit another Chesterfield. *Got to have more help. I'm awake, just as well wake everybody else up, too,* he thought and picked up the receiver. A Des Moines bureaucrat for the Iowa State Law Enforcement Agency answered. His sleep-filled voice sounded like a moan from the grave. After Goodwin told him about the planned robbery, he said he'd immediately dispatch two state agents, Burke and Schmidt. Both were reliable men and combat veterans of the German War.

Bill Frew and Lud Johnson came into the room and sat on a sofa. They gratefully accepted a cup of coffee and listened while the sheriff filled them in.

"What you need, John," Lud explained in his Swedish accent," is Doc Bay. Someone's sure to get hurt in this dust-up."

Goodwin slapped his forehead. "I should have thought of that! Honey, call Doc Bay and tell him we need him here right now and real bad."

While his wife was on the phone, Goodwin smiled at Lud. "Glad you thought of that."

Lud nodded and shut his eyes.

By four A.M., the men had all gathered in the sheriff's living room. Goodwin opened another pack of Chesterfields and thought about the strength of his crew. Grandman and Lobberden wanted the gang bad. Pershing, the site of the previous robbery, was in Marion County, and the pair had taken a lot of criticism over the previous hold-up. Bill Frew and Lud were as steady as rock walls. Doc Bay was fearless and a man of almost superhuman strength. Godwin's eyes flicked over the two state men. Schmidt was balding and had piercing blue eyes. His build reminded Goodwin of an oak tree trunk. The freckle-faced Burke was a happy-go-lucky Irishman, but he had steel in him. Goodwin sensed it. This crew would do fine.

The thought struck him from nowhere and he spoke without thinking. "We have four U.S. Springfield Army rifles in our armory. Why don't we use those, you know, put some riflemen out as flankers?"

"That's what the Army does. They would put the machine gunners in close and the riflemen out a ways on each end," Burke said. "You know four good men?" 113

"There's the Williamson brothers and Sam Scott. Then there's uh, Pat Purcel. Those four are all good squirrel hunters and vets of the Rainbow Division," Bill Frew said.

"They'd be good rifle shots and be familiar with the Springfield from the War," Burke added.

"Phone them," Goodwin pointed to Bill Frew. "Tell them they are all deputized and to come down to the jail right quick."

By the time the four volunteers arrived at the jail and got their rifles, soft light was stealing through the streets of Albia. Goodwin said it was time to go. "Yeah," someone said, "we don't want to be late."

There was a forced laugh, and the eleven armed men piled into three cars driven by the Albia police. They drove north on Highway Sixty and turned west on the Hiteman Road.

After about a quarter of a mile the shale road curved. The ground on the south fell off into a deep ditch. A tangled snarl of buckbrush and dead horseweeds crowded the verge on the north side of the road. Beyond that, the field to the north rose higher and looked down on the road.

"Pull over," Goodwin said. "Let's check this out."

Goodwin's breath plumed in the cool April air when he eased out of the car. His shoes cracked on the road's red shale. The men followed Goodwin, staying close, almost crowding him, and carrying their weapons like rabbit hunters. The sheriff scanned up and down the brush-covered ditch. Then he squinted his right eye against the sun and looked at the high ground to the north.

"This place just might work—what do you think?" he peered over his glasses at Burke who stood beside him.

"Perfect layout. We can use the ground for our advantage," Burke said. "It's your show, sheriff, how do you want to play this?"

"Well, first the Olds will come down the road heading towards Hiteman. About nine o'clock Evans will drive past us hauling the money west to the mine. Ten, fifteen minutes later, after the hold-up, the Olds will come back past us heading back towards Highway Sixty. When it's even with us, we shoot out their tires," Goodwin said.

"How are you going to deploy your men?" Burke asked,

"My idea is to place our machine gunners in the ditch at say, thirty foot intervals. Bill Frew and Lud will be down there with shotguns. Doc Bay in there with them. What do you think?" Goodwin lit another cigarette.

"What about the riflemen, Sheriff?" Schmidt asked from across the hood of the car.

"Put them up on the hill. The Williamson brothers can hunker down in that swale." Goodwin pointed to the northwest. "Sam Scott can hide behind that wagon up on the ridge line. Purcel, you go east of the wagon maybe a hundred yards. That'll get you up high enough you can see what's going on. When you see the Olds coming west off Highway Sixty, throw up your arm like you're broadcasting seed. That's the sign for us to get ready. Got it?"

"Got it," Purcel answered and fiddled with the sights of his Springfield.

"After the gang makes the heist and are coming back east towards the highway—when they get right in front of us—Purcel, you shoot out their front tire. That's our signal. We'll jump up from the ditch and cut loose with the machine guns," Goodwin said.

The men nodded their heads. Some scuffed the red shale with their feet. Goodwin saw lips move in prayer.

"One more thing. This gang doesn't kill people at holdups. So, we don't kill them either. Shoot the tires out and pray we don't have a gunfight. O.K.? Let's go. Everybody get to their posts. I want these cars out of here now," Goodwin said.

 "Watch sharp, Purcel," Sheriff Grandman said. "We're depending on you."

"Yeah, yeah, I will," Pat Purcel muttered and slung his rifle.

Purcell bulled his way through the brush-choked ditch and climbed the other side. He ripped his trousers on the new barbed-wire fence and stepped into the plowed field. The turned half-frozen earth made for hard going and he was glad he wore his work shoes. Out of sorts, he walked to the top of the hill. Sam Scott waved to him from the farm wagon that was a football field length away. The view of the area wasn't right. He walked backwards a dozen steps and found a spot that commanded a long stretch of the Hiteman Road. Below him, he could see the men in the ditch.

Purcel opened the rifle's breech and inserted a five round stripper clip of .30-06 cartridges. He worked the action and chambered a live round. The bolt handle closed with a satisfying click. From old habit, he flipped on the safety. For an instance, Purcel was transported back in time and space to 1917 and France. Heard Sergeant Lee shout, "Lock and load!" in a flashback so real, Purcel could hear the rumble of artillery and smell the stench of death. A line of German soldiers, their bayonets gleaming in the sun, ran towards him. Purcel spit out the brassy taste of fear in his mouth and shut his mind to the memories.

In time, the morning sun warmed the day. Traffic hummed on Highway Sixty and a

CAR AND WOUNDED BANDIT

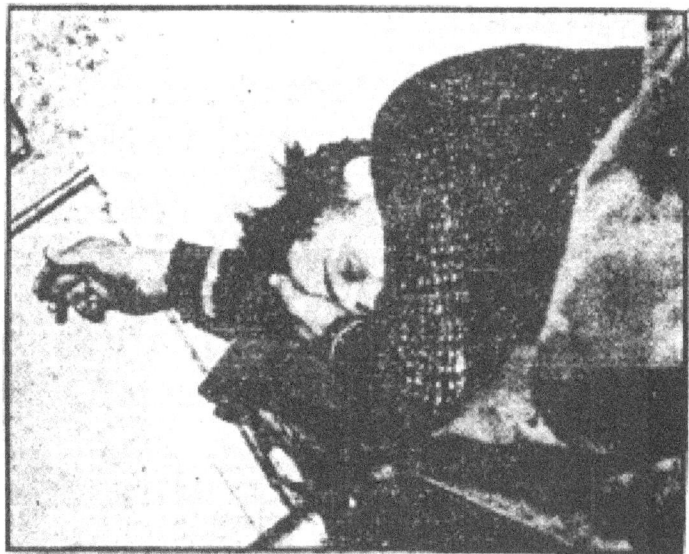

—COURTESY DES MOINES REGISTER

Shown above are two pictures taken Wednesday afternoon following the attempted theft of the Hiteman mine payroll, in which four men were captured. The upper picture is of the bandit's car, riddled by bullets from guns of the posse. The lower picture shows Ned Warner, wounded member of the bandit gang, on his cot in the Monroe county jail.

farm truck lumbered past on the Hiteman Road. Pat Purcel wore a path on the plowed field: twelve steps towards Sam Scott, do an about-face, and twelve steps back. His thoughts were jumbled. *Sandy's got the kids ready for school and covered for me at work—those big crappies are hitting at the reservoir about now—wish I had a cup of coffee.*

An eon passed, then another, and Purcel looked at his pocket watch. Eight o'clock. *Things are going to start to happen,* his mind whispered.

A black Oldsmobile turned off the highway and started down the road. Hiding his rifle at his side, Purcel made a show of walking towards the wagon, trying to give the impression of a farmer at work. The guy in the front seat of the Oldsmobile waved. Purcel smiled and waved back. The Olds rolled on, went around the curve and out of sight heading west. When the car came back, going towards the pavement, Purcel was at the wagon. He knelt down by the tailgate and pretended to be repairing it. The driver in the Olds glanced at him and drove towards Highway Sixty. After a few short words with Scott, Purcel walked back to his post.

At eight forty-five, the Olds returned. Purcel watched them drop off a man at the intersection and start down the Hiteman Road, the sunlight blinking off the car's bumper. Purcel threw his hand in the air, pantomiming a man broadcasting seed. The car zipped past the waiting lawmen and disappeared down the road. Minutes later, Evans' Chevy clattered past, leaving a fine red-shale mist on the road.

This is it! Purcel threw off his jacket and sat on it. Slipped the leather sling on his left and assumed a trained rifleman's sitting position. He drew the rifle butt into the hollow of his shoulder and laid his cheek on the walnut stock. Purcel heard nothing. He sat there Buddha-like, his mind devoid of thought. The Oldsmobile came back, traveling at a high rate of speed. Purcel took up a good sight picture and led the front tire by six feet. He squeezed the trigger, didn't hear the rifle's retort or feel the recoil. The tire exploded into a snarl of shredded rubber. Purcel cycled the Springfield and shot again. A blinding cloud of steam spouted from the radiator. Just then, the ditch erupted into a hammering racket of automatic gunfire and shotgun blasts. The car weaved, shuddered, and careened into the ditch on the south side of the road.

Purcel cheered, held the rifle at port arms and raced towards the wreck. When he got to the road, the two Marion County lawmen stood there with the other three riflemen. Below him, the Olds lay on its roof, all four tires shredded. The two Tommy-gunners were straddling a ruined fence and facing the car. Mike Bara and George Schindler crawled out of the car, their hands held high. Bill Frew and Lud Johnson slapped cuffs on them and led them up the bank. Doc Bay and Sheriff Goodwin helped the blood-splattered Ned Warner.

A bevy of police cars howled their banshee wails, and a line of cars filled the Hiteman Road. A dozen hands helped put Warner on a gurney.

"You did a great job, sheriff," Burke told him and shook his hand.

"I can take no credit for this," John Goodwin said. "Ten good men made this happen."

"It's always a good job when nobody gets killed," said Schmidt.

"Yeah, I was lucky to get out of there alive," shouted Bara.

Purcel unloaded the Springfield and handed it to Bill Frew. He started back into the field to get his jacket. *Don't think I'll work today,* he told himself. *Going to have Sandy fix me some breakfast. Too keyed up for a nap. The crappies ought to be biting at the reservoir this afternoon.*

Justice was swift in 1935. In a week, the four men were on their way to Anamosa to begin twenty-five year prison sentences.

BOB HEFFRON'S BASS POND

Somewhere south of Georgetown there is a pond that harbors the state's biggest bass, maybe a world record for all I know. I've never fished the pond. The location is top secret.

I hear there's a fallen tree that lies out on the water, and a monster bass hangs around it. Some fishermen swear they've had fifty-pound test line snapped like a thread. Other men say the fish swirled in front of them and they thought it was a shark.

I taught my buddy, Pat S., all he knows about fishing. I'm proud to say he's a master bass fisherman. He's won more bass tournaments than you can shake a stick at. It's been said he could cast out on a gravel road and catch a trophy bass.

Pat S. loves a challenge. He fished the secret pond for three hours and had no luck. Cast all around the log with his best lures. Could it be the bass was too smart for him?

Pat S. sat down in the shade and watched a squirrel run out on the floating tree trunk after a fallen hickory nut. The big bass leapt out of the water, grabbed the squirrel and went back under with a mighty splash. The squirrel disappeared, leaving only some bubbles and a cloud of blood. Pat S. sat there dumfounded.

A little later, the bass surfaced and put the hickory nut back on the log.

THE END

About the Author

Tony Humeston was born and raised in Albia, Iowa, where his father and grandfather operated a furniture store and funeral home. He is a graduate of St. Ambrose University and Dallas Institute of Mortuary Science. After forty years in business, he retired and moved back to his home town, where he writes between hunting and fishing trips. He has written four novels, and his work has appeared in magazines and other publications. This is his first book about southern Iowa.

Other books
from PBL Limited

publishing and book distribution

St. Patrick's Georgetown $24.99
Concerning Mary Ann $26.99
Holding Up the Hills $24.99
Items from the Bluegrass $19.99
JANET! $19.99
Albia Centennial (reprint) $19.99
Buxton Roots $19.99
St. Joseph Hospital $19.99
Mars Hill – A Living Legacy $24.99
Days Gone By $19.99
Coming Up Dry $19.99

***Visit our website at www.pbllimited.com
to view these and other titles.***

Please add 7 percent sales tax (Iowa residents) and $5.00 per address for mailing in the United States. Send check or money order to PBL Limited, P.O. Box 935, Ottumwa IA 52501-0935.

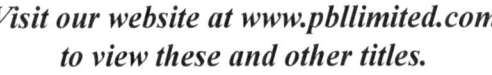

www.ingramcontent.com/pod-product-compliance
Lightning Source LLC
Chambersburg PA
CBHW080733020726
47503CB00010B/2894